THE DANCING KETTLE
and Other Japanese Folk Tales

Books by Yoshiko Uchida:

*published by Creative Arts Book Co.

The DANCING KETTLE
and Other Japanese Folk Tales

Retold by YOSHIKO UCHIDA

ILLUSTRATED BY RICHARD C. JONES

BERKELEY • 1986

CREATIVE ARTS BOOK COMPANY

This is a new edition of the book
orignally published by
Harcourt, Brace and World.

Creative Arts edition published 1986.

For information contact:
Donald S. Ellis
Creative Arts Book Company
833 Bancroft Way
Berkeley, California 94710

ISBN 0-88739-014-5
Library of Congress Catalog Card No. 86-70457

PRINTED IN THE UNITED STATES OF AMERICA

To M. and D.

PREFACE

These folk tales have not been translated literally from the Japanese versions. I have retold them in my own words, and have taken the liberty of adapting them so they would be more meaningful to the children of America.

It is my hope that along with the folk tales of other lands, they will awaken in readers the realization that all children, in whatever country they may live, have the same love of fun and a good story. I hope, too, that, in their own way, they will help to increase among our children a feeling of respect for and understanding of the cultural heritages of other countries and peoples. It is in such small and simple beginnings that I rest my hopes for the creating of "one world."

Y. U.

CONTENTS

ix

THE DANCING KETTLE

IGH up in the wooded hills of Japan, there once lived a priest in a beautiful old temple. He was a good and kindly man, and was known for his love of beautiful things. He liked especially to collect teacups and kettles, and used them often in performing the formal tea ceremony.

One day he discovered a particularly beautiful teakettle and brought it back to the temple with him.

"My, but it is lovely," he murmured as he stroked the smooth sides of the kettle. He placed it carefully on a small teakwood table, and sat back on a little cushion on the *tatami* to admire its shape and beauty.

As the old priest sat in the sunny little room looking at his precious new kettle, his head slowly began to nod . . . nod . . . nod . . . Outside, the tall pine trees swayed in the breeze and whispered softly to the priest.

Before long he was sound asleep.

Suddenly the kettle began to wiggle! Out popped a head on top. Then out came two arms, and finally two legs. With a big thud it jumped right off the table and began to dance around the room.

Just then, two other priests of the temple happened to be walking by. They tapped on the old priest's door, but, hearing no answer, pushed the sliding doors open just a tiny bit. As they peered into the room what did they see but a kettle with arms and legs dancing around the sleeping priest!

"Wh-what is this? What has happened to the kettle?" shouted one of the priests.

"Get up, sir! Get up!" shouted the other to the old priest.

The old priest grunted and shook the sleep from his eyes.

"What is all this noise? What is the trouble, my friends?" he asked.

"Look at your kettle! It's walking! It's dancing! Why, it must be haunted!" they exclaimed.

The old priest rubbed his eyes and looked at the table, but now the kettle was back in place just as it had been before.

"Ho, ho, my young friends," laughed the priest.

"What are you talking about? You must both be dreaming."

"But the kettle *was* dancing. We saw it with our own eyes," they answered as they stared at the shiny new kettle which now sat quietly on the table.

"Come, come, you interrupted my lovely afternoon nap," said the old priest, and he again closed his eyes.

The two young priests couldn't understand what had happened, and shaking their heads, they left the room.

That night the old priest filled his new kettle and decided to boil some water for tea. He placed it on the little *hibachi* in his room and sat down to wait for the water to boil. Suddenly the kettle shouted, "Help! This is hot!" Out came its legs and off it hopped onto the floor.

The old priest was so surprised he could scarcely believe his eyes. "Help! Help!" he called. "This kettle is alive!"

His friends quickly rushed to his room and caught the dancing, hopping kettle, but when they had it in their hands, it was just an ordinary teakettle. There were no arms or legs to be seen.

"What have I bought?" asked the old priest sadly. "Surely it must be an evil thing, for it is no ordinary teakettle. I will give it to the junkman tomorrow."

And so early the next morning the old priest gave his teakettle to the junkman.

"Why, this is a beautiful kettle," said the junkman. "I shall keep it for myself," and he carried it home, whistling a happy little tune.

That night as he sat admiring the kettle, it again sprouted a head and two arms and two legs. It jumped off the table and began to dance around the surprised junkman.

"My goodness! What sort of creature are you anyway?" he asked.

"Why, I am a very, very special kind of a teakettle. If you take good care of me, I can be very useful to you, but you must not fill me with water and put me over a fire like other pots and pans. Do you think you can feed me once in a while, and take good care of me?" asked the kettle.

"Of course, of course I can," answered the man. He was still so surprised, his eyes looked like two round balls. "Tell me more about yourself," he added.

"When I was in the temple I had a terrible time. They would not feed me, and the old priest filled me with water and put me over glowing coals. Oh, I shudder to think of it," sighed the kettle. "Now if you know how to care for me, I can bring you much good luck. Did you know that I can dance and sing and do all sorts of fancy tricks?"

"Did you say you can dance and sing and do tricks?" asked the junkman. "Why, we could start a little theater out in the streets. People would pay money to see a tea-kettle that can dance, and then I would be able to feed you well, and take very good care of you too. What do you think of that?"

"A fine idea! A lovely idea! Here, I will dance for you right now," said the kettle, and with a clinkety-clank and a skip and a hop it pranced about the junkman as he sang and clapped his hands.

The kettle and the junkman worked together for many days and at last they were ready to open their little street theater. The junkman pasted signs and post-ers about the streets of the town, telling everyone to come to see the dancing kettle. Then at night he stood beside his little theater shouting, "Come one, come all! See a teakettle that can dance and sing! Come see a ket-tle that can do tricks!"

Soon little children and their mothers and fathers, and sisters and brothers, and aunts and uncles, and grand-mothers and grandfathers came streaming out to see the kettle dance and sing. The children laughed and clapped their hands in glee as the kettle danced about the little stage.

People from villages near and far came to see this strange teakettle, and one day the kettle decided it would do something even more wonderful than just dancing or singing. It crossed the stage of the little theater balanced on a tightrope strung high up in the air. When the people saw this, they shouted and clapped their hands, and threw gold coins onto the stage. Soon so many people wanted to see the kettle that they crowded and squeezed and pushed, even for a tiny glimpse.

Each day the junkman fed the kettle well and took good care of it. Each night he counted the gold coins that the people threw, and slowly the shiny golden stacks grew higher and higher.

"My, we are fast becoming rich," he said to the kettle with a big smile. But the junkman was not a greedy person, and when he had saved a little money he said to the kettle, "You must be growing tired of dancing and singing every day, and I certainly have all the money I want now. Wouldn't you like to stop dancing and spend a quiet and peaceful life?"

"Oh, yes, indeed I would," said the kettle. "You are a good and kind man, my friend."

And so they closed their little street theater and decided to live quietly and peacefully.

As the junkman thought about the success which the kettle had brought him, he suddenly remembered the old priest who had given it to him.

"Why, I must go to thank the priest," he thought. "And I have an excellent idea!" So one bright, sunny morning when the skies were blue and clear, he decided to set out on his visit. He carefully polished the tea-kettle and wrapped it in a gay, bright *furoshiki*. He then put on his very best clothes, put half of all the money he had earned into a leather pouch, and started up the wooded hillside to the temple.

When he arrived at the temple, the priest was surprised to see him.

"What brings you here, my friend?" asked the priest.

So the junkman told the priest all about his wonderful kettle and of the street theater which he had.

"And I have you to thank for all my success," he added, "for if you hadn't given me the kettle all this would never have happened. I have brought half of my earnings for the temple, and I shall return the kettle to you, for it is really yours. I know you will take good care of it, and I am sure it will be happier here in this beautiful temple where others may come to admire its beauty."

"You are a generous and good man, my friend," said

the priest. "Surely you will be blessed with many happy days, and we shall always remember you here in the temple."

"Take good care of my friend, the teakettle, won't you?" called the junkman as he was leaving.

"Indeed we will," the priest called back, as he watched the junkman walk slowly into the pine trees and down the wooded slope.

And indeed he did take good care of the little teakettle. Never again did the old priest try to boil water in it. He placed it carefully on his beautiful teakwood table, where many people who had heard of the dancing kettle came to admire it. From that day on, the kettle had a very special place in the temple, and it lived happily and peacefully ever after.

URASHIMA TARO AND THE PRINCESS OF THE SEA

URASHIMA TARO AND THE
PRINCESS OF THE SEA

LONG, long ago, in a small village of Japan, there lived a fine young man named Urashima Taro. He lived with his mother and father in a thatched-roof house which overlooked the sea. Each morning he was up before the sun, and went out to sea in his little fishing boat. On days when his luck was good, he would bring back large baskets full of fish which he sold in the village market.

One day, as he was carrying home his load of fish, he saw a group of shouting children. They were gathered around something on the beach and were crying, "Hit him! Poke him!" Taro ran over to see what was the matter, and there on the sand he saw a big brown tortoise. The children were poking it with a long stick and throwing stones at its hard shell.

"Here, here," called Taro. "That's no way to treat him! Why don't you leave him alone, and let him go back to the sea?"

"But we found him," said one of the children. "He belongs to us!"

"Yes, yes, he is ours," cried all the children.

Now, because Urashima Taro was a fair and kindly young man, he said to them, "Suppose I give each of you something in return for the tortoise?" Then he took ten shiny coins out of a small bag of money and gave one to each child. "Now, isn't that a fair bargain?" he asked. "A coin for each of you, and the tortoise for me."

"Yes, yes. Thank you!" called the children, and away they ran to the village candy shop.

Taro watched the old tortoise crawl away slowly toward the sea and called, "You'd better stay at home in the sea from now on, old fellow!" Then, smiling happily because he had been able to save the tortoise, he turned to go home. There his mother and father were waiting for him with bowls of steaming rice and soup.

Several days passed, and Taro soon forgot all about the tortoise whom he had saved. One day he was sitting in his boat feeling very sad because he could catch no fish. Suddenly he heard a voice from the sea calling,

"Urashima-san! Urashima-san!"

"Now who could be calling me here in the middle of the sea?" thought Urashima Taro. He looked high and low, but could see no one. Suddenly, from the crest of a big wave, out popped the head of the old tortoise.

"I came to thank you for saving me the other day," said the tortoise.

"Well, I'm glad you got away safely," said Taro.

"This time I would like to do something for you, Urashima-san," said the tortoise. "How would you like to visit the princess who lives in the Palace of the Sea?"

"The princess of the sea!" shouted Taro. "I have heard often of her beauty, and everyone says her palace is more lovely than any place on earth! But how can I go to the bottom of the sea, and how can I enter her palace?"

"Just leave everything to me," said the old tortoise. "Hop on my back and I will see that you get there safely. I will also take you into the palace, for I am one of the palace guards."

So Urashima Taro jumped onto the smooth round back of the tortoise, and away they went. Swish, swish . . . the waves seemed to part and make a path for them as the tortoise swam on. Soon Taro felt himself going down . . . down . . . down . . . into the sea, but he wasn't getting wet at all. He heard the waves lapping gently about his ears. "That's strange," thought Taro. "This is just like a dream—a nice happy dream."

Before long, they were at the bottom of the big blue sea. Taro could see bright-colored fish playing hide and seek among the long strands of swaying seaweed. He could see clams and other shellfish shyly peeking out at him from their shells. Soon Taro saw something big and shiny looming in the hazy blue water.

"Is that the palace?" he asked anxiously. "It looks very beautiful."

"Oh, no," answered the tortoise. "That is just the outer gate."

They came to a stop and Taro could see that the gateway was guarded by a fish in armor of silver. "Welcome home," the guard called to the tortoise, as he opened the gate for them to enter.

"See whom I have brought back with me," the tortoise answered happily. The guard in the armor of silver turned to Urashima Taro and bowed most politely. Taro just had time to return the bow when he looked up and saw another gate. This one was even larger than the first, and was made of silver stones and pillars of coral. A row of fish in armor of gold was guarding the second gate.

"Now, Urashima-san, if you will get off and wait here, I will tell the princess that you have come," said the tortoise, and he disappeared into the palace beyond the gate. Taro had never seen such a beautiful sight in all his life. The silver stones in the gate sparkled and glittered as though they were smiling at him. Taro had to blink hard.

Soon the tortoise was back at his side telling him that the princess was waiting to see him. He led Taro through the gate of coral and silver, and up a path of golden stones to the palace. There in front of the palace stood the beautiful princess of the sea with her ladies-in-waiting.

"Welcome to the Palace of the Sea, Urashima Taro," she said, and her voice sounded like the tinkling of little silver bells. "Won't you come with me?" she asked.

Taro opened his mouth to answer, but not a sound would come forth. He could only look at the beautiful princess and the sparkling emeralds and diamonds and rubies which glittered on the walls of the palace. The princess understood how Taro felt, so she just smiled kindly and led him down a hallway paved with smooth, white pearls. Soon they came to a large room, and in the center of the room was an enormous table and an enormous chair. Taro thought they might have been made for a great king.

"Sit down, Urashima-san," said the princess, and as he

sat in the enormous chair, the ladies-in-waiting appeared from all sides. They placed on the table plate after plate of all the delicious things that Taro could think of. "Eat well, my friend," said the princess, "and while you dine, my maids will sing and dance for you." Soon there was music and singing and dancing. The room was filled with laughing voices. Taro felt like a king now! He thought surely this was all a dream, and that it would end soon. But no, after he had dined, the princess took him all through the beautiful palace. At the very last, she brought him to a room that looked as though it were made of ice and snow. There were creamy pearls and sparkling diamonds everywhere.

"Now, how would you like to see all the seasons of the year?" whispered the princess.

"Oh, I would like that very much," answered Taro, and as he spoke, the east door of the room opened slowly and quietly. Taro could scarcely believe the sight before his eyes. He saw big clouds of pale pink cherry blossoms and tall green willow trees swaying in the breeze. He could hear bluebirds singing, and saw them fly happily into the sky.

"Ah, that is spring," murmured Taro. "What a lovely sunny day!" But before he could say more, the princess led him further on. As she opened the door to the south,

Taro could see white lotus blossoms floating on a still green pond. It was a warm summer day, and he could hear crickets chirping lazily, somewhere in the distance. She opened the door to the west and he saw a hillside of maple trees. Their leaves of crimson and yellow were whirling and dancing down among golden chrysanthemums. He had seen such trees each fall in his own little village. When the princess opened the door to the north, Taro felt a blast of cold air. He shivered, and looked up to see snowflakes tumbling down from gray skies. They were putting white caps on all the fence posts and treetops.

"Now you have seen all the seasons of the year," said the princess.

"They were beautiful!" sighed Taro happily. "I have never seen such wonderful sights in all my life! I wish I could stay here always!"

Taro was having such a very good time that he forgot all about his home in the village. He feasted and danced and sang with his friends in the Palace of the Sea, and before he knew it, three long years had gone by. But to Taro they seemed to be just three short days.

At last Taro said to the princess, "Alas, I have been here much too long. I must go home to see my mother and father so they will not worry about me."

"But you will come back?" asked the princess.

"Oh, yes, yes. I will come back," answered Taro.

"Before you go I have something for you," said the princess, and she gave Taro a small jewel box studded with many precious stones.

"Oh, it is beautiful, Princess," said Taro. "How can I thank you for all you have done for me?"

But the princess went on, "There is just one thing about that box," she said. "You must never, never open it if you ever wish to return to the Palace of the Sea. Can you remember that, Urashima Taro?"

"I will never open it, no matter what happens," promised Taro. Then he said good-bye to all his friends in the palace. Once again he climbed on the back of the old tortoise and they sailed toward his village on the seacoast. The princess and her ladies-in-waiting stood at the coral gate and waved to Taro till he could no longer see them. The tortoise swam on and on, and one by one all the little bright-colored fish that had been following them began to turn back. Before long, Taro could see the seacoast where he used to go fishing, and soon they were back on the very beach where Taro had once saved the tortoise. Taro hopped off onto the smooth white sand. "Good-bye, old friend," he said. "You have been very good to me. Thank you for taking me to the most beautiful place I have ever seen."

"Farewell, Urashima-san," said the old tortoise. "I hope we may meet again some day." Then he turned and crawled slowly back into the sea.

Now that he was in his own village once more, Taro was most anxious to see his parents. He ran along the path which led to their house with his jewel box tucked securely under his arm. He looked up eagerly at each person whom he passed. He wanted to shout a greeting to them, but each face seemed strange and new. "How odd!" thought Taro. "I feel as though I were in some other village than my own. I don't seem to know anyone. Well, I'll soon see Mother and Father," he said, and hurried on. When he reached the spot where the house should have been, there was no house to be seen. There was just an empty lot full of tall green weeds. Taro couldn't believe his eyes. "Why, what has happened to my home? Where are my parents?" he cried. He looked up and down the dusty path and soon saw an old, old woman coming toward him. "I'll ask her what has happened to my home," thought Taro.

"Old woman, please, can you help me?" asked Taro.

The old woman straightened her bent back and cocked her gray head, "Eh, what did you say?" she asked.

"Can you tell me what happened to Urashima Taro's

home? It used to be right here," said Taro.

"Never heard of him," said the old woman, shaking her head.

"But you must have," Taro replied. "He lived right here, on this very spot where you are standing."

"Now let me see," she sighed. "Urashima Taro. Yes, it seems I have heard of him. Oh, I remember now. There is a story that he went out to sea in his fishing boat one day and never came back again. I suppose he was drowned at sea. Well, anyway, that was over three hundred years ago. My great-great-grandfather used to tell me about Urashima Taro when I was just a little girl."

"Three hundred years!" exclaimed Taro. His eyes were like saucers now. "But I don't understand."

"Well, I don't understand what you want with a man who lived three hundred years ago," muttered the old woman, and she trudged on down the road.

"So three years in the Palace of the Sea has really been three hundred years here in my village," thought Taro. "No wonder all my friends are gone. No wonder I can't find my mother or father!" Taro had never felt so lonely or so sad as he did then. "What can I do? What can I do?" he murmured to himself.

Suddenly he remembered the little jewel box which the princess had given him. "Perhaps there is something in there that can help me," he thought, and forgetting the promise he had made to the princess, he quickly opened the box. Suddenly, there arose from it a cloud of white smoke which wrapped itself around Taro so that he could see nothing. When it disappeared, Urashima Taro peered into the empty box, but he could scarcely see. He looked at his hands and they were the hands of an old, old man. His face was wrinkled; his hair was as white as snow. In that short moment Urashima Taro had become three hundred years older. He remembered the promise he had made to the princess, but now it was too late and he knew that he could never visit the Palace of the Sea again. But who knows, perhaps one day the old tortoise came back to the beach once more to help his friend.

THE EIGHT-HEADED DRAGON

THE EIGHT-HEADED DRAGON

LONG, long ago when gods and goddesses ruled over the land of Japan, there lived a god called Prince Susano. He was a handsome young lad, but a very mischievous one too. He played pranks on many of the gods and goddesses, but he especially liked to play tricks on his sister, the beautiful goddess of the sun, who sent warmth and light to the people of the earth.

The goddess of the sun was very patient with her brother, and tried not to be angry with him. One day, however, he frightened away her handmaiden, who sat weaving a piece of bright-colored cloth, and then destroyed the beautiful loom on which she had been working.

"This time you have done something for which I cannot forgive you," she said sadly to her brother, and without another word she shut herself inside a big, dark cave on a high hillside. With her into the cave she took all the light and warmth she usually sent down to earth, and soon all the land was in darkness.

When the gods and goddesses saw what Prince Susano had done, they shouted angrily, "Punish him quickly for his wicked deed," and it was decided that he should be sent forth from the land of the gods, never to return. The gods then turned to the hillside to beg the goddess of the sun to come out of the cave.

"The people of the earth will have to spend the rest of their days in darkness," they cried to the goddess of the sun. "And soon they will all perish!"

When she heard their pleas she could no longer stay in hiding. She stepped out of the dark cave and once again the earth was covered with her warm sunshine. The gods and goddesses sighed with relief and smiled happily, but still they would not forgive Prince Susano.

The young god felt very sad indeed, but he knew that he deserved to be punished. He left the land of the gods quietly, and set out for the province of Izumo. Soon he came to a little stream which flowed merrily through a fresh green meadow. As he sat at the edge of the stream and watched the water bubble over the pebbles, he noticed a pair of red chopsticks floating down the stream.

"Oh-ho, a pair of chopsticks!" he cried. "That means someone must be living nearby," and he quickly got up and walked in the direction from which the chopsticks had come.

Soon he spied a little wooden cottage. An old man, an old woman, and a young girl sat in front of the house. Something was very, very wrong, however, for all three of them had their heads in their hands and were crying bitterly.

"Here, here, what is the matter?" called Prince Susano.

"Oh, we are very, very sad," moaned the old man, "for tonight we must lose our only and beloved daughter."

"But why is that?" asked the prince.

"You see, we once had eight other lovely and beautiful daughters, but now they are all gone, and we have only the maid who sits beside us. The eight-headed dragon of the forest has eaten all the others, and tonight he is coming to take our last one. Alas, alas, then we shall be all alone," sobbed the old man and woman, and they cried as if their hearts would break.

"That is a very sad story, indeed," said Prince Susano. "I shall kill this eight-headed monster so your last daughter can be saved."

"Oh, no, kind sir," said the old man quickly. "You are very kind to offer to kill this dragon for us, but you see, he is no ordinary dragon. He has eight heads, as I have mentioned before, and he is as long as eight valleys laid end to end. He will surely kill you before you can even strike the first blow."

"His eight heads do not frighten me," said the prince. "After all, he is only a dragon, and I am a god!"

"A god!" the old man exclaimed in surprise.

"Yes, I am the brother of the goddess of the sun," explained Prince Susano.

"Oh, a thousand pardons," replied the old man humbly. "Surely, if you are a god, you will have no trouble slaying a dragon, even an eight-headed one."

"We would be so grateful if you could kill this monster for us," added the old woman. "We could never repay you if you would just save our last daughter from the terrible fate of her sisters."

"Of course," said Prince Susano. "But we must get to work quickly. Bring me eight jugs, and fill them full of wine," he requested the old man.

When the old man brought the eight jugs, the prince carefully placed them at the foot of a big boulder which stood at the mouth of the stream.

"Now then," he said to the daughter, "you must climb up on the boulder and sit in such a way that your face will be reflected in all eight of the jugs of wine. You must sit very still, even though the dragon comes and you are very frightened."

"Oh, I shall do anything to help you slay the dragon," answered the young girl.

That evening she climbed on top of the boulder and sat very still so that her face was reflected in all eight jugs of wine. Prince Susano then hid behind another boulder nearby. Soon the sun slipped behind the hills and the sky grew darker and darker. A round full moon moved up among the stars and cast a soft silvery light on the hillside. The two waited very quietly—the girl on the boulder and the prince behind another.

The prince looked toward the dark forest, and finally he saw sixteen balls of fire glowing in the darkness. They looked like bright red berries growing on the dark bushes, but he soon saw that they were the sixteen eyes which shone from the eight heads of the monstrous dragon. They came closer and closer, and grew larger and larger. The prince could hear the dragon breathing heavily as he crawled slowly up to the big boulder. Eight red tongues lapped hungrily from the eight huge heads.

Now the dragon spied the eight jugs of wine. He looked with hungry eyes, and when he saw the face of the girl reflected in each jug, he thought he saw eight lovely maidens sitting in eight jugs of wine. Eagerly he thrust all eight heads into the jugs and began to drink the sweet wine. "How good the eight lovely maidens taste," he thought. Now the dragon did not know that the prince had mixed some poison with the wine in each jug. When the dragon had finished drinking all the wine, the poison made him very sleepy. He grunted and groaned, his eight heads drooped, and with a great crash he toppled over.

Slowly the prince came from behind the boulder. He pulled out his sword and ran toward the sleeping dragon. The dragon raised his eight heads and bared his ugly fangs at the prince, but he was too weak to fight. So the prince quickly chopped off the eight heads, and just to make certain that the dragon was dead, he chopped up his body with his long sword. When he got to the dragon's tail he raised his sword high for one last blow. As it came down on the dragon's tail there was a loud clank. "That's strange," thought the prince, and he quickly slit the tail open. There he saw a beautiful sparkling silver sword. Its hilt was studded with emeralds and rubies and pearls. He took it out carefully, and later carried it safely to the ruler of the land. There it was placed in a vault for safekeeping, and became one of the most prized possessions of the land.

Everyone, near and far, heard of the prince's courage in killing the eight-headed dragon. Even in the far-away land of the gods, the gods and goddesses heard what the prince had done. They nodded their heads and agreed that he deserved to be pardoned for the trick he had played on the sun goddess' handmaiden.

Prince Susano did not return to the land of the gods, however. He went instead to the land of Izumo, to the home of the old man and woman. There he married the lovely daughter whom he had saved from the eight-headed dragon, and they all lived happily for many, many years after.

THE OLD MAN WITH THE BUMP

THE OLD MAN WITH THE BUMP

LONG, long ago, there lived an old man who had a large bump on his right cheek. It grew larger and larger each day, and he could do nothing to make it go away.

"Oh, dear, how will I ever rid myself of this bump on my cheek," sighed the old man; and though he went from doctor to doctor throughout the countryside, not one of them could help him.

"You have been a good and honest man," said his wife. "Surely some day there will be someone who can help you."

And so, the old man kept hoping each day that this "someone" would come along soon.

Now one day the old man went out into the hills to collect some kindling for his fire. When the sun began to dip behind the hills, he strapped a large bundle of wood on his back and slowly began the long walk back to his little house at the foot of the hill. Suddenly the sky began to darken, and soon huge drops of rain splashed down on the wooded hillside. The old man hurriedly looked about for some shelter, and before long spied a gnarled old pine tree with a large hollow in its trunk.

"Ah, that will be a good shelter for me during the storm," he said to himself, and he quickly crawled into the hollow of the tree. He did this just in time too, for soon the rain poured down from the skies as though someone had overturned an immense barrel of water up in the heavens. The old man crouched low as the thunder crashed above his head and the lightning made weird streaks of light in the dark forest.

"My, what a storm this is!" he said to himself, and closed his eyes tight. But it was just a thundershower, and it stopped as suddenly as it had begun. Soon, all the old man could hear was the drip, drop . . . drop . . . of the rain slipping down from the shiny pine needles.

"Ah, now that the rain has stopped I must hurry home, or my wife will worry about me," said the old man.

He was about to crawl out of the hollow of the tree, when he heard a rustling like the sound of many, many people walking through the forest.

"Well, there must have been other men caught in the forest by the storm," he thought, and he waited to walk home with them. But suddenly the old man turned pale as he saw who was making the sounds he had heard. He turned with a leap, and jumped right back into the hollow of the tree. For the footsteps weren't made by men at all. They were made by many, many ghosts and spirits walking straight toward the old man.

The old man was so frightened he wanted to cry out for help, but he knew no one could help him.

"Oh, dear, ohhhh, dear," moaned the old man, as he buried his head in his hands. "What will they do to me?"

But soon he raised his head ever so slightly, for he thought he heard music in the air. Yes, there were singing voices and laughing voices floating toward him. The old man lifted his head a little more and ever so carefully took a peek to see what they were doing. His mouth fell wide open in surprise at the sight before his eyes. The spirits were gaily dancing about on the soft carpet of pine needles. They laughed and sang as they whirled and twirled about. They were feasting, and drinking, and making merry.

"A feast of spirits! My, I have never seen such a strange

sight," said the old man to himself. Soon he forgot to be afraid and he poked his head further and further from the hollow of the tree. The old man's feet began to tap in time to the music, and he clapped his hands along with the spirits. His head swayed from side to side and he smiled happily as he watched the strange sight before him.

Now he could hear the leader saying, "Such foolish dances! I want to see some really fine dancing. Is there no one here who can do any better?"

Before he knew what he was doing, the old man had jumped right out of the hole, and danced out among the ghosts.

"Here, I will show you something different! I will show you some fine dancing," he called. The spirits stepped back in surprise and the old man began to dance before them. With so many spirits watching him, the old man did his very best, and danced as he had never danced before.

"Good, very good indeed," said the leader of the spirits, nodding his head in time to the music.

"Yes, yes," agreed the others. "We have never seen such fine dancing!"

When the old man stopped, the spirits crowded about him, offering him food and drink from their feast.

"Thank you, thank you," said the old man happily. He breathed a sigh of relief as he saw that he had pleased the spirits, for he had feared that they might harm a mortal such as he.

The leader of the spirits then stepped before the old man and said in a deep, low voice, "We would like to see more of such fine dancing. Will you return again tomorrow, old man?"

"Yes, yes, of course I will come," answered the old man, but the other spirits shook their ghostly heads and lifted warning fingers.

"Perhaps this mortal will not keep his word," they protested. "Let us take a forfeit from him—something which he treasures most—then he will be sure to return for it tomorrow."

"Ah, a fine plan indeed," answered the leader. "What shall we take from him?"

All the spirits stepped around the old man, and examined him from head to toe to see what would make a good forfeit.

"Shall it be his cap?" asked one. "Or his jacket?" asked another.

Then finally one spoke up in a loud and happy voice, "The bump on his cheek! The bump on his cheek! Take that from him and he will be sure to come for it tomorrow, for I have heard that such bumps bring good luck to human beings, and that they treasure them greatly."

"Then that shall be the forfeit we will take," said the leader, and with one flick of his ghostly finger he snatched away the bump on the old man's cheek. Before he could say Oh the spirits had all disappeared into the dusky woods.

The old man was so surprised he scarcely knew what to do. He looked at the spot where the spirits had just been standing and then rubbed the smooth, flat cheek where once the bump had been.

"My goodness! My, my," murmured the old man. Then with a big smile on his face he turned and hurried home.

Now the old woman had been very worried, for she was afraid that the old man had met with an accident during the storm. She stood in the doorway of their cottage waiting for him to return, and when at last she saw him trudging down the road, she hastened to greet him.

"My, but I was worried about you," she said. "Did you get drenched in that thundershower?" Then suddenly the old woman stopped talking and looked carefully at the old man.

"Why, wh-hy, where is the bump on your right cheek? Surely you had it this morning when you went out into the woods!"

The old man laughed happily and told the old woman all about his meeting with the spirits. "So you see, I have lost my bump at last!" he added.

"My, isn't that nice!" exclaimed the old woman, admiring the old man's right cheek. "We must celebrate this happy occasion," she said, and together they feasted with *akano gohan* and *tai*.

Early the next morning they heard a knock on their door, and there stood the greedy man who lived next door to them. He had come to borrow some food, as he so often did.

Now this man also had a bump on his cheek, but his was on the left side of his face. When he saw the old man without his bump, he threw up his hands in surprise and exclaimed, "Why, what has happened? Where is the bump on your face?" He peered closely at the old man's face and said, "How I would like to get rid of mine too! Perhaps I can if I do exactly as you did." Then, because he wanted the same good fortune, he asked anxiously, "Tell me, exactly what did you do?"

So the old man carefully explained how he hid in the hollow of an old tree until the spirits came to dance in the dusk. Then he told about the dance he did for them and how they took his bump for a forfeit.

"Ah, thank you, my friend," said the neighbor. "Tonight I shall do exactly the same thing." And after borrowing a large sack of the old man's rice, he hurried home.

That evening, the greedy neighbor trudged out into the woods and found the same tree. He slipped into the hollow trunk and waited quietly, peeking out every once in a while to watch for the spirits. Just as the sky began to darken and the setting sun painted all the clouds in gold, the spirits again twirled and whirled out into the small clearing in front of the old tree.

The leader looked about and said, "I wonder if the old man who danced for us yesterday will soon be here?"

"Yes, yes. Here I am!" called the greedy neighbor, as he leaped from the hollow tree trunk. He opened out a fan and then he began his dance. But alas and alack, this old man had never learned how to dance. He hopped from one foot to the other, and shook his head from side to side, but the spirits were not smiling as they had been the day before. Instead they scowled and frowned, and called out, "This is terrible. We have no use for you, old man. Here, take back your precious bump," and with a big THUMP the leader flung the bump on the greedy man's right cheek. Then the spirits disappeared into the woods just as quickly as they had come.

"Ohhhhh!" cried the greedy man as he sadly walked home. "Never again will I try to be someone else."

Now he not only had a big bump on his left cheek, he had one on his right cheek too. And so the greedy man who had tried to copy his neighbor went home looking just like a chipmunk with both cheeks full of nuts!

THE RABBIT AND THE CROCODILE

THE RABBIT AND THE
CROCODILE

LONG ago, near the province of Inaba in Japan, there was a small island called Oki. On this island lived a little white rabbit. He often grew lonely on his island, and his one wish was to get to the mainland of Inaba, but a long span of sea stretched between him and the land he wished to visit. Each day he would stand at the water's edge, shade his eyes with his white paw, and gaze longingly toward Inaba.

"Some day I shall get over there," he would say to himself.

Now one day, as he stood on the beach of the island of Oki, he saw a big crocodile swimming lazily toward his island. The rabbit was so happy to see someone he could talk to that he hopped about merrily on the sand. Suddenly he had an idea. "Why, that crocodile could help me get to the province of Inaba," he thought to himself. "I shall ask him as soon as he comes up on my island." He waited impatiently for the crocodile to climb up on the warm sand. Then he had still another idea. "I mustn't let that fellow see how anxious I am to get to Inaba," he thought. "For then he may not take me. No, I shall be very clever. I shall trick him into taking me there without knowing what he is doing." The rabbit smiled to himself to think how he would fool the big crocodile who was three times as large as he was.

"Hello there, Mr. Crocodile!" he called. "Isn't it a fine day?"

"Indeed it is," answered the crocodile. "But you seem to be lonely all alone on this little island."

"Oh, no, I'm not the least bit lonely," said the rabbit. "But why don't you stay and talk with me for a little while?"

So the rabbit and the crocodile sat on the sunny beach of the island of Oki and talked of many things.

Before long the rabbit said, "Mr. Crocodile, your home is in the deep sea yonder, and my home is here on land. I wonder which of us has more friends, you or I?"

"Why, I have more, of course," answered the crocodile. "You have only the friends who live on this tiny island, while I have a whole sea full of friends. There's no question who has more friends!" laughed the crocodile.

The rabbit smiled to himself. His plan was working out just as he wished. But when he turned to the crocodile, he looked surprised and said, "Do you really have so many friends, Mr. Crocodile? Do you have so many friends that if they all lay side by side, they would reach from this beach to the land of Inaba?"

"Of course I do," said the crocodile. "I could easily find enough friends in the sea to stretch from here to Inaba. Wait a few minutes and I'll just show you," and with a big splash he swam off into the sea.

The rabbit sat quietly on the beach and waited patiently for the crocodile to return. Soon he saw dozens of black specks swimming toward his island. As they grew bigger and bigger, he could see that they were dozens and dozens of crocodiles returning with his friend.

"Look at this, Mr. Rabbit," called the crocodile happily. "I have enough friends to reach from here to China!"

"Well, you do have a lot of friends, don't you?" said the rabbit. "But let me see if they really will reach from here to Inaba."

So the crocodile and all his friends formed one long

chain. They lay side by side in the sea, until soon they made a bridge from the island to the very shore of Inaba.

"My goodness," said the rabbit, when he saw what the crocodiles had done. "This is really a sight to see. Now let me count your friends to see how many you have. I'll just hop on each crocodile as I count him."

Then he hopped from the back of one crocodile to another. "One"—hop—"Two"—skippety-hop—"Three" —hoppity-skip—"Four—oops, you almost dropped me. Now please don't wiggle or I'll slip right off your backs," he called to the crocodiles. Then with a few more skippety-hops and hoppity-skips, he had hopped all the way across the bridge of crocodiles, from the island of Oki to the province of Inaba. When at last he reached the shore of Inaba, he sat on the beach and shook with laughter.

"Ha, ha, ha, you silly crocodile," he called to his friend. "I tricked you and all your friends into making a nice long bridge for me, and here I am at last in Inaba. Run along back to the sea now, for I won't need you any longer. Ho, ho, ho," he laughed, hopping about on the sand.

When the crocodile heard this, he was so angry his eyes flashed like two glowing coals. "You dared to trick me and my friends into becoming a bridge for a little rabbit like you!" he shouted. The crocodile hurried onto the beach and ran toward the rabbit. Before the rabbit could get away, the crocodile had snatched him, and in a minute had pulled all the fur from his body. "This is to punish you for the trick you played on me," he said angrily. Then without another word, the crocodile turned and swam off into the sea.

The little rabbit was so sad, he could do nothing but sit on the beach and cry. After a while he heard some voices nearby. It was a group of gods who were traveling through the province of Inaba.

"Why are you crying, little rabbit?" asked one of the gods.

The rabbit raised his head and said sadly, "I just had a quarrel with my friend, the crocodile, and he pulled off all my lovely white fur. Oh-h-h dear, I don't know what to do," wailed the rabbit.

Now one of the gods was a very unkind god, and he was the first to speak up. "I know how you can get well, little rabbit," he said. "Go into the sea and cover your body with the nice, cool, salty water. Then come out onto the sand and let the wind blow on your body until it is all dry."

"Thank you, I shall try that," said the rabbit, and the

gods went off down the road.

The rabbit quickly ran to the sea and did just as he had been told, but the salty water pricked his body as if a thousand bees were stinging him.

"Ohhhhh, ohhhhh," moaned the little rabbit as he jumped out of the water and rolled about on the sand. "What shall I do? What shall I do?" he cried sadly.

Soon he heard another voice calling to him. "What is the matter, little rabbit? What has happened to you?"

This time the rabbit would not answer, for he remembered how unkind the gods had been to him a few moments ago. He just kept rolling about on the sand and crying bitterly.

"If you will tell me what's wrong, perhaps I will be able to help you." This voice sounded so kind and gentle that at last the rabbit looked up and told his story.

"I played a trick on my friend, the crocodile," sobbed the rabbit. "I tricked him and his friends into becoming a bridge for me so I could come to the land of Inaba from the island of Oki. Then he was so angry with me that he pulled all the fur from my body. Just a few minutes ago, some gods passed by and gave me some very unkind advice. They told me to wet myself in the salty sea, and instead of getting better, I have grown much worse, as you can see."

"Alas, you poor creature, those gods who just passed by were my older brothers," said this god. "They did a very cruel thing to you, but on the other hand, you did a very unkind thing to the crocodile and his friends."

"Yes, yes, I know I have been very bad," said the rabbit, "and I promise I shall never do such a thing again. Now please tell me what I can do to have lovely white fur on my body once more."

"Very well," said the god kindly. "I think you have been punished enough for what you have done. Now I shall tell you how you can get well once more."

The rabbit sat up, straightened his long ears, and listened very quietly.

"Go to the lake beyond the beach, and wash off all the salt from your body," explained the god carefully. "Then find the cat-tails that grow beside the water and pick enough to make a soft mat on which you can lie. After you lie on them for a while, you will soon be like your old self again. Now hurry along," said the god. "I'll be waiting for you here on the beach."

The little rabbit went hopping along the road to the lake just as fast as he could go. He did exactly as the god had told him, and then lay down on the soft cat-tails. Soon, all the pain had gone away, and when he looked down at his body it was covered with lovely soft white fur once more. The little rabbit was so happy, he scurried back to the beach to find the god.

"I see you are all well again," said the god.

"Oh, I am indeed, thanks to your kind help." replied the rabbit happily. "I don't know what I would have done without you. Pray tell me, what are you doing here in Inaba? And, goodness me, if those gods were your brothers, you must be a god too!"

"Yes, I am," smiled the god. "You see, we are all on our way to try to win the hand of the princess who lives in Inaba. Being the youngest in our family, I had to carry our bags, and that is why I am so far behind the others. I must hurry along now, or I shall be too late."

"I can't believe that those unkind gods can be the brothers of anyone as kind and gentle as you," said the rabbit, shaking his head. "Surely the princess will want to choose you and not your unkind brothers."

The god laughed and gave the rabbit a pat on the shoulders. "Well, we shall see, little friend," he called. Then he swung the bags over his shoulder and went off down the road to the town of Inaba.

"Good-bye, and thank you again," called the rabbit as he watched the kind god going off toward the town.

And just as the little rabbit had hoped, the princess did wait until the kind god arrived, and she did choose him instead of any of his unkind brothers. It is said that the god and the beautiful princess lived happily ever after, and somewhere in the land of Inaba, the little white rabbit lived happily too.

THE JEWELS OF THE SEA

THE JEWELS OF THE SEA

ONCE long, long ago in the land of Japan, there lived two young princes. The older prince was an excellent fisherman whose skill no one could ever equal. It was said that he could catch anything that swam in the sea. Now the younger prince was as skilled on land as his brother was at sea. He was the finest hunter in all the land, and feared no animal that stalked through the woods and over the mountains of Japan. Each day the two set out together; the older brother would go toward the sea with his rod and reel, while the younger brother with his bow and a quiver full of arrows set forth for the mountains.

Now one morning as the two princes prepared to go out for the day, the younger brother said, "Each day for many years we have done the very same thing. You go to the sea and I to the mountains. I have grown weary of the same sport each day. Wouldn't you like to go hunting in my place today, while I go fishing in yours?"

"A good idea," said his brother. "I will take your bow and arrow and you shall take my rod and reel. Take care how you use them, however, for they are my most prized possessions."

So the older prince headed for the mountains and the younger prince for the sea. When the young prince reached the edge of the sea, he sat down among some boulders. He baited his hook with clumsy fingers, threw it into the water, and anxiously waited for the fish to bite. Each time the line moved just a little, he pulled it up to see what he had caught, but each time the hook came up empty. Finally the sun began to sink slowly below the rim of the mountains, but still he had not caught a single fish. What's more, he had even lost his brother's very best hook.

"I must find my brother's hook," thought the young prince sadly, and he searched among the crevices of the boulders, and on the sands of the beach. As he was looking for the lost hook, his brother came back from the mountains. He too was empty-handed, for although he was an excellent fisherman, he could not hunt game.

"What are you looking for?" he called crossly to his younger brother.

"I have lost your precious hook," said the young prince, "and I have searched everywhere but cannot find it."

"Lost my hook?" shouted the older brother. "You see, this is what comes of your idea to change tasks for the day. If it hadn't been for your foolish idea, this never would have happened. You are a clumsy, blundering fool, and I shall not return your bow and arrow to you until you find my hook."

The young prince was very sad, and spent long hours searching for the lost hook. At last he began to think he would never find it by the sea, so he took his very best sword and broke it into hundreds of tiny pieces. Then he made five hundred beautiful hooks for his brother with the tiny pieces of his sword. He brought these to his brother saying, "Since I cannot find your lost hook, I have broken my sword and made five hundred new hooks for you. Please forgive me for having lost your precious hook."

But his older brother would not forgive him. The young prince made five hundred more hooks, but still his brother would not forgive him. He only said, "Even though you bring me a million hooks, I will not forgive you until you return the one hook you lost!"

So once again the young prince went to the seashore

to see if the tide might have washed the lost hook up onto the sand. He roamed about sadly, walking back and forth along the beach where he had fished. Suddenly, from nowhere, there appeared an old man with hair as white as the clouds in the sky.

"Pray tell me, what is the young prince doing all alone, and why do you look so sad?" asked the old man.

So the young prince told him how he had lost his elder brother's hook, and how he could never be forgiven until he found it again.

"But, my dear prince," said the old man kindly. "Surely your lost hook is at the bottom of the sea by this time, or at least in the belly of a fish. You will never find it here on the shore."

"Then what can I do?" asked the young prince.

"Why, the only thing you can do is to go to the King of the Sea and ask him to help you find it," answered the old man.

"That is an excellent idea!" said the prince. "But how will I ever get to his palace at the bottom of the sea?"

"Just leave everything to me," replied the old man. "I will help you get to his palace."

And so the old man made the prince a very special boat which could take him safely to the bottom of the sea. He then told him just how to get there, and wished him luck in finding his lost hook.

"Thank you, old man. You shall surely be rewarded when I return," said the young prince, and he sailed off for the palace of the King of the Sea.

He followed the old man's directions carefully, and before long he saw the sapphire roofs of the palace sparkling in the blue water. A large gate guarded the entrance, and the prince found it was locked tight.

"Oh, dear, how will I get in?" he thought as he looked around. Then he spied a lovely old tree growing by the gate. Its gnarled branches bent low and hung over a beautiful silver well.

"I shall just climb up on one of those branches and rest awhile," thought the prince. "Then someone may come along through the gates soon."

So he climbed up on one of the low branches and sat down to rest. Before long, the big gate of the palace slowly swung open. The prince looked down quickly and saw two beautiful maidens coming out of the gate carrying a lovely golden cup. They hurried toward the well and bent down to fill their cup with the clear, cool water. As they looked into the mirror-like water, they both cried out, for there, reflected in the stillness, was the face of the young prince.

They looked up at the tree in surprise, and saw the

prince sitting quietly on one of the branches.

"I didn't mean to startle you," he said to the two maidens. "I have come a long way and just wanted to rest for a few minutes. I am very thirsty, and I see that you have a lovely golden cup. Will you give me a drink of water?"

"Why, of course," answered the two beautiful maidens.

When the prince had had his fill of water, he pulled a precious stone from a chain around his neck and dropped it into the golden cup before he returned it.

"Thank you for your kindness," he said. "I am looking for the King of the Sea. I wonder if you could help me find him?"

"Oh, but of course," answered the two lovely maidens, laughing gaily. "For we are his daughters!"

They hurried to tell their father of this strange visitor whom they had found sitting on the branch of the old tree by the well.

"Surely he is no ordinary mortal, for look at this beautiful stone which he dropped into our cup. It seems to be a *maga-tama*, a stone which is worn only by royalty."

The King of the Sea then called the young prince into his most beautiful room. "Now tell me what I can do for you," he said to the prince.

So the young prince told him who he was, and why he had come. He told him how he had lost his brother's hook and had come down to the bottom of the sea to seek help.

"Will you be good enough, kind sir, to search your kingdom for my brother's fishhook?" he asked.

"By all means, my good friend, by all means," replied the king, and he beckoned to one of his servants. "Call together all my subjects who live in the kingdom of the sea," he said.

The servant disappeared for a few moments and before long, all who lived in the great kingdom of the sea came swimming toward the palace of their king: giant tortoises and little clams; sea horses, crabs, and lobsters with long green claws; mackerels, sea bass, herrings, swordfish, and all the many, many fish in the sea. When they had all gathered in the great courtyard, the king stood before them and called out,

"We have a very important visitor with us today—a prince who has come down to the bottom of the sea to search for a lost fishing hook. If any among you have seen it, speak now and tell your king!"

The fish looked at each other and shook their shiny heads; the tortoise looked at the clam and slowly shook his head; the crabs and lobsters wriggled their feelers and looked about on the sand and in the coral. At last, from far back in the group a little silver fish came forward and spoke to the king.

"Oh, good King, I do believe it is my friend, the red snapper, who has swallowed the hook of our visiting prince."

"And why do you say that?" asked the king.

"Because, sir, he has been complaining of a sore throat and has eaten nothing for a long time. And you see, he is not present now, for I fear he is ill at home."

"Hmm, that *is* strange," said the king, "for the red snapper is usually the first to come to all our gatherings. Have him brought forth immediately."

Soon the red snapper was brought to the meeting. He looked pale and sickly, and his tail drooped on the sand.

"Yes, sir?" he answered in a low, weak voice. "Did you wish to see me?"

"Why did you not come when I called the fish of my kingdom?" asked the king.

"Because, sir, I have been very ill," moaned the red snapper. "I haven't been at all well for some time. My throat is sore, I cannot eat, and see—my fins will not stand up on my back. I fear something is very wrong indeed."

"He's swallowed the hook! He's swallowed the hook!"

murmured all the fish of the sea.

"Then open his mouth and look," commanded the king. Two guards immediately opened wide the red snapper's mouth, and peered down his throat. There they found the prince's shiny hook, and quickly removed it. The red snapper smiled happily, and so did the young prince. He thanked the guards and the king and all the subjects of the Kingdom of the Sea, for now at last he had recovered his brother's precious hook. Now at last his task was completed and he could return home once more. But the Kingdom of the Sea was so beautiful, and he was having such a pleasant time that he stayed on and on. Before he quite realized it, three long years had gone by. At last he went to the King of the Sea and said,

"I have spent three long and happy years here in your lovely Kingdom of the Sea, but I cannot stay forever. I must return to my own kingdom and to my own land above the waters."

The king turned to the young prince and said, "I hope that you of the land and we of the sea shall always be friends. As a token of our friendship, I wish you to take back with you two jewels of the sea." Then he called his servant, who came in with two large and beautiful jewels. They sparkled and glistened as the king held them in his hands.

The king raised the jewel in his right hand and said, "This stone has the power to call forth the waters of the sea. Raise it above your head and great waves will come rushing up about you no matter where you may be."

Then the king held up the jewel in his other hand. "Raise this stone above your head and no matter how high the seas that surround you may be, the waters will recede and be drawn away." Then he gave the two jewels to the prince.

"They are beautiful jewels, sir," said the prince. "And what wonderful powers they possess!"

"Keep them with you always," said the king, "and they will protect you from all danger and harm."

The prince thanked the good king and prepared to be on his way. He said farewell to his many friends in the Kingdom of the Sea, and then the king called a large alligator who was to carry the prince back again to land. This was an even stranger vessel than the one which had brought him to the bottom of the sea, but the alligator swam swiftly and smoothly, and soon the prince was standing safely on the very beach from which he had departed.

He hurried to his palace and holding the hook which he had found, he called to his older brother, "Here I am, back once again, and here is your precious hook at last!"

Now the older brother had seized the throne while the younger prince was away, thinking that his younger brother would never return. He was very happy that he alone was the great and powerful ruler of the land, so when the young prince appeared with the lost hook, he was not at all glad to see him. Dark and evil thoughts cropped up in his jealous mind, and soon he decided that he would kill his younger brother so that he could continue to be the only ruler of the land.

One day as the young prince was strolling about in the fields outside the palace, the older brother crept up behind him with a long dagger. He raised it high in the air and was about to stab the young prince. But the young prince turned quickly and remembered what the King of the Sea had told him. He reached for the jewels of the sea and raised one high over his head. At once great high waves came thundering over the fields. They crashed and roared about the older prince and swept him off his feet.

"Help, help, I'm drowning! Save me, save me!" he cried.

The young prince then reached for the other jewel and held it high over his head. The waters immediately began to recede and the waves rolled gently back again toward the sea. The older brother sat on the ground gasping for breath.

"Thank you for saving my life," he said to the young prince. "You must have a power far greater than I, to be able to command the waters of the sea to come and go when you choose. I have done you a great injustice and I hope you will forgive me."

The kind young prince was quick to forgive his older brother and before long they were once again the best of friends. From that day on, they ruled together over a land of peace and plenty.

THE PRINCESS OF LIGHT

ONCE upon a time, there was an old man and an old woman who lived in a small village in Japan. Their little wooden house with the low thatched roof stood nestled against a hillside covered with trees. Each day the old man strapped his straw sandals on his feet and went out to the nearby bamboo thicket to cut down long, slender stalks of bamboo. When he brought them home, the old woman would help him cut and polish the smooth stalks. Then together they would make bamboo vases, baskets, flutes, and many beautiful ornaments which they could sell in the village.

They were good, kind, and honest people, and they worked very hard. They were happy, but they were lonesome, for they had no children. Both of them wanted a child more than anything else in the world.

"Oh, if only we had a little boy or a little girl, how happy we would be," sighed the old man.

"Yes, wouldn't that be wonderful!" answered the old woman. "I would rather have a child than all the riches on earth!"

And so each day they both knelt at the little shrine in the corner of their room, and prayed that some day they would be granted a child.

Now one day when the old man went out into the bamboo thicket, he saw one stalk which was shining so brightly it looked as though it were made of gold. He hurried toward it and looked at it closely, but he could not tell what made it shine.

"My, what a strange bamboo," said the old man to himself. "Perhaps I'd better see what is inside." So he began to cut it down with the saw which he carried at his side. But suddenly he stopped, for he heard something very strange!

"What was that?" asked the old man. "It sounded like the crying of a baby!"

He straightened his back and looked all around, but he did not see anyone. All he could see were the stalks of bamboo swaying gently in the breeze.

He shook his head slowly and said, "My, I must be getting old to be hearing such strange sounds in a bamboo thicket."

He was turning again toward the shining bamboo when he heard the sound once more. He was sure this time that it was a baby crying, and the sound came right from inside the strange shiny stalk. Quickly he cut down the bamboo and looked inside the hollow of the stalk. There he saw a tiny baby girl! She looked up at the old man and smiled sweetly. And the old man was so surprised at this strange sight, he blinked hard and touched the little girl to see if she were real.

"My goodness! Good gracious! Oya-oya!" was all the old man could say. "This child must have been sent to us straight from heaven," he thought, as he picked her up very carefully. Then he quickly started homeward, for he could scarcely wait to show her to the old woman.

When the old woman saw the beautiful child, she threw up her hands in surprise. "God has been good to us!" she exclaimed. "We must take very good care of our little girl." Then she hurriedly set about spreading a quilt on the floor where she gently laid the new baby.

The next morning the old man was up bright and early. He whistled gaily as he walked toward the bamboo thicket. As he came closer to the spot where he had found the little baby the day before, he saw another bamboo which was shining brightly.

"I wonder if I will find another little baby," thought the old man, as he prepared to cut down the bamboo. He listened for any sound that might be the crying of a child, but he heard only the song of a sparrow as it flew into the thicket. This time, when he cut down the shiny bamboo stalk, a shower of gold coins fell to the ground. They glittered and sparkled, and seemed to tell the old man, "Take us home. We are yours!" The old man gathered up the coins and filled his moneybag. Then he hurried home once more, chuckling softly to himself to think how he would again surprise his wife.

When the old woman saw the coins, she said, "My, how lucky we are! Perhaps this is God's way of helping us provide for our little daughter. We must be grateful and take good care of her."

"Yes, yes, we shall always work hard and take good care of our child," said the old man.

From that day on, each time the old man went out to the bamboo thicket, he found one shiny golden stalk. When he cut it down, he always found the hollow filled with gold coins. Before long the old man and woman became rich, but they continued to work hard.

The little baby of the bamboo was a wonderful child indeed. Each night she seemed to grow a whole year older, instead of just a day older. Each morning she surprised the old man and woman by being able to do or say something new.

"My, but she is a bright child," said the old woman.

"And see how much more beautiful she becomes each day," added the old man.

As she grew older, they discovered something even more wonderful about her. A beautiful, bright light seemed to glow all around her, just like the light which the old man had seen around the bamboo in which he found her. So the old man and woman decided to call their lovely daughter Kaguya Hime, which means Princess of Light. Their little home seemed to be filled with golden sunlight day and night, and they no longer had to use the lamps in the evening.

Kaguya Hime continued to grow in beauty each day, until soon the whole countryside had heard of her loveliness and of the radiant glow which she cast about her.

"She is like a lovely golden sunbeam," said some. "She is like sunshine on a rainbow," said others. "She is an angel from heaven," said still others; and everyone who knew her came to love her dearly.

One day as the old man sat in front of his house, he saw three young men coming up the path toward him.

"Now what can I do for you, my friends?" asked the old man. "Have you come to look at my bamboo vases and baskets?"

"Oh, no, sir," said the first young man. "We have come for something far more important."

"Ho, ho!" laughed the old man. "I think I know why you have come. You wish to meet my daughter, Kaguya Hime, is that not so?"

"We wish to do more than that," replied the second young man.

"We wish to marry her!" added the third young man.

"Well, well!" exclaimed the old man. "That is very nice, but she cannot marry all three of you! Let us call Kaguya Hime herself, and let her choose among you."

The three young men were very worried, for each one wished more than anything else to be the one whom Kaguya Hime would choose.

The old man called his lovely daughter and told her about the three young men. "Which one will you choose, my dear?" asked the old man.

"Alas, it is difficult for me to choose," said Kaguya Hime, as she smiled at the three young men. "Suppose I say that I shall marry the first of them who can bring me what I want most."

"And what is it that you want most?" asked the three young men anxiously.

Kaguya Hime's eyes sparkled, and the glow around her

seemed even brighter than usual. She spoke as though she were dreaming of a far-off fairyland, and said, "First, I want the pearl which hangs about the neck of the great dragon of the sea. Then, I want a *kimono* of silk that fire can never destroy. Lastly, I would like to have a cherry tree that blossoms all the year round."

"Oh, beautiful Kaguya Hime," said the three young men, "we will comb the earth for each of these things that you wish to have. We will not return until we have found them." And so the three young men hurried off to begin their search.

The first young man went off to the sea to capture the great dragon with the pearl about his neck. He sailed out in a little wooden vessel and searched all the dark, wet caves along the coast of Japan, but nowhere could he find any sign of the dragon. Then he turned away from the old familiar shores, and sailed far out into the blue waters. Those who watched him from the shore saw his boat grow smaller and smaller, until it was a tiny black speck on the horizon. Day after day his friends waited and watched for him to return, but the weeks turned to months, the months to years, and he never came back. And so the first young man never came back to the home of Kaguya Hime.

Now the second young man went in search of a

kimono of silk that fire could not destroy. He went to every town and village for miles around, searching out the great silk merchants of Japan. At last he came upon a merchant who told him that he had just one such dress that would not burn even if it were thrown into flames.

"Give it to me quickly!" shouted the young man. "I will buy it from you at any price!" Then he gave the merchant all the money he had and quickly returned to the home of Kaguya Hime. He proudly showed her the beautiful silk *kimono* and waited anxiously to hear what she would say.

"Oh, it is very beautiful indeed," said Kaguya Hime, as she gently stroked the silky folds of the dress. "Are you sure that fire cannot destroy it?"

"That is what the merchant told me," said the young man. "Let us test it with flames to see if that is really true."

So Kaguya Hime carried it to the stove where a pot of rice was cooking. She opened the door and tossed the dress on the burning wood. The young man held his breath, wondering if the silk could really withstand the fire. But as the red flames reached the silk dress, it turned to silver-white ashes and disappeared at the bottom of the stove.

"I have been tricked! The wicked merchant was not

telling the truth," shouted the young man angrily. "Alas, now I have neither the dress of silk that would not burn, nor a cent of my savings. I am a pauper and cannot ask you to marry me," he added sadly. Then he left the home of the old man and woman, knowing that he could never win Kaguya Hime.

The third young man had gone in search of a cherry tree that would bloom all through the year. He wandered over hill and dale, collecting cherry trees from all the land. He gave them the very best of care, and when spring came, he was rewarded with beautiful pink blossoms on all his trees. As spring turned to summer, however, he could do nothing to keep the blossoms on the trees. One by one they floated away with the breeze. The young man was so discouraged, he went to the wise old man of his village and asked for his help.

"Alas, my son," said the wise old man. "Trees are very much like people. We cannot dance and play in party clothes all year long. There are times when we must wear somber colors, when we must work and sleep. It is the same with trees; they cannot remain in bloom always, and you will never find such a tree—at least not in this world."

And so the third young man gave up the search, and he too knew that he could never return to ask for the hand of Kaguya Hime.

As word spread throughout the land of the difficulty the three young men had in trying to win Kaguya Hime, other young men grew too discouraged to try, and soon no one came to ask if he might marry lovely Kaguya Hime.

One day, however, the prince of the land heard about this beautiful maiden who made such difficult demands of all the men who wished to marry her.

"I must see her for myself," said the dashing young prince, and he prepared to have her sent before him.

When Kaguya Hime heard of this she was very sad, for she knew that she could not refuse to marry the prince. She knew that instead she must go far away, for she could never marry anyone on earth. She went to her mother and father and said, "The time has come for me to return to my home."

"But you are in your own home right now," replied the old man and woman.

"Yes, this is my home on earth," said Kaguya Hime. "But you see, my real home is in heaven. I was sent to you to be your daughter, but I was told I could never marry any of the young men of this earth. You see now why I made it so difficult for the three who wished to marry me. Now I must return to heaven before the prince sends for me." She kissed the old man and woman gently and said, "Thank you for being such good and kind parents to me. Then she stepped to the door, where the old man and woman could see a beautiful golden cloud waiting for her. Before they could call out to her, she stepped onto the cloud, waved her hand in farewell, and vanished into the golden mist. The cloud rose swiftly and quietly into the blue sky and disappeared into the sunset beyond the hills.

The old man and woman were so surprised, they could scarcely speak. "Just imagine, she was an angel from heaven!" whispered the old man. "How lucky we were to have had such a wonderful daughter, even for such a short time!"

"Ah, yes," sighed the old woman. "She was a princess straight from heaven!"

Then, hand in hand, the old man and woman slowly went back to their little work table to polish bamboo once again. They were lonely, but they no longer wished and prayed that they would be granted a child, for they could always remember lovely Kaguya Hime. And though they were a little sad, they both smiled, for they knew that when they went to heaven they would see Kaguya Hime standing there waiting for them.

THE WEDDING OF THE MOUSE

THE WEDDING OF THE MOUSE

ONCE upon a time, there lived in the deep, dark cellar of a large mansion a very wealthy and prosperous mouse. Now he had a daughter named Chuko whom he thought was the most beautiful, intelligent, and graceful mouse in the whole country.

"Why, she is so fair and so lovely, only the greatest being in this whole wide world would be worthy of her," he said to his wife. "We must search far and wide until we find just the right person to marry our Chuko."

Mother Mouse sat down and cocked her little gray head. Father Mouse sat down and whisked his long gray whiskers. "Now who is great enough to marry our lovely daughter?" they both thought to themselves.

Suddenly Father Mouse smiled happily. "I have it!" he cried. "The greatest being in all this world is the bright sun who sends down his rays to keep us warm and to help the rice in the fields to grow. It shall be the sun who marries our beautiful Chuko."

"Yes, yes, that is an excellent idea," agreed Mother Mouse. "Go quickly and ask the sun if he will marry our daughter."

So that very day, Father Mouse put on his best clothes and scampered out to see the great sun.

"Oh, Mr. Sun, Mr. Sun," he called. "Our daughter, Chuko, is so beautiful and so lovely she must marry the greatest being on this earth. You are big and bright; your warm rays bring us light each day and help the rice to grow in the fields. We think you are greater than anyone else in this world, and would like you to marry our beautiful daughter."

The sun smiled and sent bright golden beams scattering through the air. "Ah, my good friend," he said. "I am not the greatest being on earth. There is someone who is even greater than I."

"But who can that be?" asked Father Mouse.

"Look over there at those white clouds," said the sun. "Soon they will scurry across the sky and cover me with a soft white blanket and you will no longer be able to see me. You see, I am powerless when Mr. Cloud comes to hide me."

"Alas, then I must seek Mr. Cloud, for he is even

greater than you," said Father Mouse, and off he scampered to see the cloud.

"Oh, beautiful cloud up in the blue sky, you are greater than the sun itself, for you can hide the sun so it can no longer shine. I have come to ask if you will marry my daughter, Chuko, for she must marry the greatest being on this earth."

"Yes, I can hide the sun, and the moon too, but I am not the greatest. There is someone greater and more powerful than I."

"More powerful than you, Mr. Cloud? Pray tell me who that may be," asked Father Mouse.

"Why, it is the wind, for when Mr. Wind comes and huffs and puffs, he can blow me wherever he wishes. You see, he is greater than I," said Mr. Cloud.

"Then it is the wind who is greatest," said Father Mouse, and off he went in search of the wind that blew gently through the tall pine trees.

"Oh, great wind," he said. "Mr. Cloud can hide the sun and the moon, but you are even greater than the cloud, for when you huff and puff you can scatter the cloud wherever you wish. You are the greatest being on this earth, and I have come to ask if you will marry my beautiful daughter."

"Thank you, Mr. Mouse, but I am not as great as you

think," whistled the wind, "for when I come up against Mr. Wall, I cannot blow him down no matter how hard I blow."

"Ah, then the wall is greater than you, Mr. Wind," said Father Mouse. "Farewell then, for I cannot rest until I find the greatest being in this world." And off he ran back to the big mansion.

"Mr. Wall, Mr. Wall," cried Father Mouse. "You are the greatest being on this earth, for the wind can scatter the clouds that can hide the sun or moon, but he can never blow you down. You shall be the one to marry my beautiful Chuko."

"Now just a moment, Mr. Mouse," said the wall. "Yes, I am stronger than the wind, for he cannot blow me down no matter how hard he tries. I have no trouble stopping Mr. Wind, but there is someone I can never stop."

"Someone that even you cannot stop, Mr. Wall? Now who could that be?" asked Father Mouse.

"Why, it's the little mouse himself!" laughed the wall. "When mice come to nibble at me and make holes in my sides, I can do nothing to stop them."

"My goodness," cried Father Mouse. "Then the mouse is the greatest being on earth!" He happily hurried toward home so he could tell Mother Mouse the good news.

When he got home, Mother Mouse was waiting anxiously. "Did you find a good husband for our lovely Chuko?" she asked.

"I have some wonderful news for you, my dear," said Father Mouse, smiling happily. "We mice are greater than anyone else on earth!"

"My, my, that *is* good news," said Mother Mouse. "But tell me, how did you learn that?"

"You see, I thought the sun was the greatest, but he really isn't at all, for he can do nothing when Mr. Cloud wraps him up in a blanket of white. Now Mr. Cloud is not the greatest either, for when Mr. Wind comes whistling along he can send Mr. Cloud scurrying wherever he wishes across the sky."

"Then surely Mr. Wind is greatest," said Mother Mouse.

"No, no, for when Mr. Wind comes up against Mr. Wall he can go no further. Then Mr. Wall told me that there is someone even he cannot stop, and that is the mouse who can nibble holes right through his sides. So you see," said Father Mouse, "the mouse is the greatest of all. We shall marry Chuko to a mouse."

"A fine idea, Father. A very fine idea," said Mother Mouse.

"And I think it is a fine idea, too," said Chuko, who had been sitting quietly all this time listening to her father's story.

And so beautiful little Chuko married the fine young mouse who lived next door. All the mice from near and far came to see the beautiful wedding, and all agreed that it was quite the loveliest wedding they ever did see. And of course, they both lived very happily ever after.

MOMOTARO: BOY-OF-THE-PEACH

MOMOTARO: BOY-OF-THE-PEACH

ONCE long, long ago, there lived a kind old man and a kind old woman in a small village in Japan.

One fine day, they set out from their little cottage together. The old man went toward the mountains to cut some firewood for their kitchen, and the old woman went toward the river to do her washing.

When the old woman reached the shore of the river, she knelt down beside her wooden tub and began to scrub her clothes on a round, flat stone. Suddenly she looked up and saw something very strange floating down the shallow river. It was an enormous peach; bigger than the round wooden tub that stood beside the old woman.

Rumbley-bump and a-bumpety-bump . . . Rumbley-bump and a-bumpety-bump. The big peach rolled closer and closer over the stones in the stream.

"My gracious me!" the old woman said to herself. "In all my long life I have never seen a peach of such great size and beauty. What a fine present it would make for the old man. I do think I will take it home with me."

Then the old woman stretched out her hand just as far as she could, but no matter how hard she stretched, she couldn't reach the big peach.

"If I could just find a long stick, I would be able to reach it," thought the old woman, looking around, but all she could see were pebbles and sand.

"Oh, dear, what shall I do?" she said to herself. Then suddenly she thought of a way to bring the beautiful big peach to her side. She began to sing out in a sweet, clear voice,

> "The deep waters are salty!
> The shallow waters are sweet!
> Stay away from the salty water,
> And come where the water is sweet."

She sang this over and over, clapping her hands in time to her song. Then, strangely enough, the big peach slowly began to bob along toward the shore where the water was shallow.

Rumbley-bump and a-bumpety-bump . . . Rumbley-bump and a-bumpety-bump. The big peach came closer and closer to the old woman and finally came to a stop at her feet.

The old woman was so happy, she picked the big peach up very carefully and quickly carried it home in her arms. Then she waited for the old man to return so she could show him her lovely present. Toward evening the old man came home with a big pack of wood on his back.

"Come quickly, come quickly," the old woman called to him from the house.

"What is it? What is the matter?" the old man asked as he hurried to the side of the old woman.

"Just look at the fine present I have for you," said the old woman happily as she showed him the big round peach.

"My goodness! What a great peach! Where in the world did you buy such a peach as this?" the old man asked.

The old woman smiled happily and told him how she had found the peach floating down the river.

"Well, well, this is a fine present indeed," said the old man, "for I have worked hard today and I am very hungry."

Then he got the biggest knife they had, so he could

cut the big peach in half. Just as he was ready to thrust the sharp blade into the peach, he heard a tiny voice from inside.

"Wait, old man! Don't cut me!" it cried, and before the surprised old man and woman could say a word, the beautiful big peach broke in two, and a sweet little boy jumped out from inside. The old man and woman were so surprised, they could only raise their hands and cry out, "Oh, oh! My goodness!"

Now the old man and woman had always wanted a child of their own, so they were very, very happy to find such a fine little boy, and decided to call him "Momotaro," which means boy-of-the-peach. They took very good care of the little boy and grew to love him dearly, for he was a fine young lad. They spent many happy years together, and before long Momotaro was fifteen years old.

One day Momotaro came before the old man and said, "You have both been good and kind to me. I am very grateful for all you have done, and now I think I am old enough to do some good for others too. I have come to ask if I may leave you."

"You wish to leave us, my son? But why?" asked the old man in surprise.

"Oh, I shall be back in a very short time," said Momotaro. "I wish only to go to the Island of the Ogres, to rid the land of those harmful creatures. They have killed many good people, and have stolen and robbed throughout the country. I wish to kill the ogres so they can never harm our people again."

"That is a fine idea, my son, and I will not stop you from going," said the old man.

So that very day, Momotaro got ready to start out on his journey. The old woman prepared some millet cakes for him to take along on his trip, and soon Momotaro was ready to leave. The old man and woman were sad to see him go and called, "Be careful, Momotaro! Come back safely to us."

"Yes, yes, I shall be back soon," he answered. "Take care of yourselves while I am away," he added, and waved as he started down the path toward the forest.

He hurried along, for he was anxious to get to the Island of the Ogres. While he was walking through the cool forest where the grass grew long and high, he began to feel hungry. He sat down at the foot of a tall pine tree and carefully unwrapped the *furoshiki* which held his little millet cakes. "My, they smell good," he thought. Suddenly he heard the tall grass rustle and saw something stalking through the grass toward him. Momotaro blinked hard when he saw what it was. It was a dog as big as a calf! But Momotaro was not frightened, for the dog just said, "Momotaro-san, Momotaro-san, what is it you are eating that smells so good?"

"I'm eating a delicious millet cake which my good mother made for me this morning," he answered.

The dog licked his chops and looked at the cake with hungry eyes. "Please, Momotaro-san," he said, "just give me one of your millet cakes, and I will come along with you to the Island of the Ogres. I know why you are going there, and I can be of help to you."

"Very well, my friend," said Momotaro. "I will take you along with me," and he gave the dog one of his millet cakes to eat.

As they walked on, something suddenly leaped from the branches above and jumped in front of Momotaro. He stopped in surprise and found that it was a monkey who had jumped down from the trees.

"Greetings, Momotaro-san!" called the monkey happily. "I have heard that you are going to the Island of the Ogres to rid the land of these plundering creatures. Take me with you, for I wish to help you in your fight."

When the dog heard this he growled angrily. "Grruff," he said to the monkey. "*I* am going to help Momotaro-san. We do not need the help of a monkey such as you! Out of our way! Grruff, grruff," he barked angrily.

"How dare you speak to me like that?" shrieked the monkey, and he leaped at the dog, scratching with his sharp claws. The dog and the monkey began to fight each other, biting, clawing, and growling. When Momotaro saw this he pushed them apart and cried, "Here, here, stop it, you two! There is no reason why you both cannot go with me to the Island of the Ogres. I shall have two helpers instead of one!" Then he took another millet cake from his *furoshiki* and gave it to the monkey.

Now there were three of them going down the path to the edge of the woods. The dog in front, Momotaro in the middle, and the monkey walking in the rear. Soon they came to a big field and just as they were about to cross it, a large pheasant hopped out in front of them. The dog jumped at it with a growl, but the pheasant fought back with such spirit that Momotaro ran over to stop the dog. "We could use a brave bird such as you to help us fight the ogres. We are on our way to their island this very day. How would you like to come along with us?"

"Oh, I would like that indeed, for I would like to help you rid the land of these evil and dangerous ogres," said the pheasant happily.

"Then here is a millet cake for you, too," said Momotaro, giving the pheasant a cake, just as he had to the monkey and the dog.

Now there were four of them going to the Island of the Ogres, and as they walked down the path together, they became very good friends.

Before long they came to the water's edge and Momotaro found a boat big enough for all of them. They climbed in and headed for the Island of the Ogres. Soon they saw the island in the distance wrapped in gray, foggy clouds. Dark stone walls rose up above towering cliffs and large iron gates stood ready to keep out any who tried to enter.

Momotaro thought for a moment, then turned to the pheasant and said, "You alone can wing your way over their high walls and gates. Fly into their stronghold now, and do what you can to frighten them. We will follow as soon as we can."

So the pheasant flew far above the iron gates and stone walls and down onto the roof of the ogres' castle. Then he called to the ogres, "Momotaro-san has come to rid the land of you and your many evil deeds. Give up your stolen treasures now, and perhaps he will spare your lives!"

When the ogres heard this, they laughed and shouted. "HO, HO, HO! We are not afraid of a little bird like you! We are not afraid of little Momotaro!"

The pheasant became very angry at this, and flew down, pecking at the heads of the ogres with his sharp, pointed beak. While the pheasant was fighting so bravely, the dog and monkey helped Momotaro to tear down the gates, and they soon came to the aid of the pheasant.

"Get away! Get away!" shouted the ogres, but the monkey clawed and scratched, the big dog growled and bit the ogres, and the pheasant flew about, pecking at their heads and faces. So fierce were they that soon the ogres began to run away. Half of them tumbled over the cliffs as they ran and the others fell pell-mell into the sea. Soon only the Chief of the Ogres remained. He threw up his hands, and then bowed low to Momotaro. "Please spare me my life, and all our stolen treasures are yours. I promise never to rob or kill anyone again," he said.

Momotaro tied up the evil ogre, while the monkey, the dog and the pheasant carried many boxes filled with jewels and treasures down to their little boat. Soon it was laden with all the treasures it could hold, and they were ready to sail toward home.

When Momotaro returned, he went from one family to another, returning the many treasures which the ogres had stolen from the people of the land.

"You will never again be troubled by the Ogres of

Ogre Island!" he said to them happily.

And they all answered, "You are a kind and brave lad, and we thank you for making our land safe once again."

Then Momotaro went back to the home of the old man and woman with his arms full of jewels and treasures from Ogre Island. The old man and woman were so glad to see him once again, and the three of them lived happily together for many, many years.

THE PIECE OF STRAW

THE PIECE OF STRAW

LONG ago, in the land of Yamato, there was a poor young man who lived all alone. He had no family to care for him, and no friends to whom he might go for help. Each day he watched his purse grow slimmer and slimmer, for there was no one who would give him work. Finally, one day, he saw that his money was almost gone.

"Alas, what am I to do?" he sighed. "The only one who can help me now is the Goddess of Mercy at the Hase Temple."

So the poor young man hurried to the temple and knelt before the shrine of the Goddess of Mercy.

"Oh, Kannon-Sama," he said. "I am without food or money, and I cannot find work to keep myself alive. I shall kneel here before your shrine until you show me some way in which I can save myself."

The young man sat very still and waited for some sign from the Goddess of Mercy. "Show me in a dream just what I am to do," he pleaded. And the young man did not move from his place before the shrine. He sat there through the long night and all the next day, and still he had no dream. He sat there for many more days and nights, but still the goddess did not help him.

At last the priests of the temple noticed the young man who neither ate nor slept, but sat quietly in front of the shrine. "He will surely starve to death if he stays there much longer," they said to each other.

Then one of the priests went to question the young man.

"Who are you, my good fellow?" he asked. "And why do you sit here for so many days and nights?"

"Alas, I have no friends nor family," said the young man sadly. "And since no one will give me work, I am also without food and money. I have come here to ask the help of the Goddess of Mercy, but if she does not help me soon, I know that I shall die here before her shrine."

Now the good priests of the temple felt great pity for the poor young man, and decided they would take turns bringing him food and water so he would not starve to death. So with their help, the young man continued to sit before the shrine for many more days and nights. He was growing sad and weary, and began to think perhaps the kind goddess would not help him after all.

At last, on the twenty-first day, as his head nodded with weariness and sleep, he thought he saw a faint dream. An old, old man with a long flowing beard seemed to be coming out of the goddess' shrine. The old man stood before him and told him to leave the temple quickly. "The very first thing that your hand touches after you leave the temple will bring you much good fortune," the old man said to him. "So keep safely whatever it is, no matter how small it may be." And then the old man faded away just as quickly as he had appeared. The young man rubbed his eyes and looked around. The Goddess of Mercy was smiling down at him, just as she had for the last twenty-one days.

"Ah, that dream was her message to me," thought the young man, and he quickly prepared to leave the temple. The priests gave him some food to take along, and the young man hurried out through the temple gates. Just as he was about to turn onto the road, he tripped over a stone and fell flat on the dirt road. As he hastened to pick himself up, he saw that he was grasping a single piece of straw in his right hand. He started to throw it away, but he suddenly remembered what the old man had said to him in his dream—"The first thing that your hand touches after you leave the temple will bring you much good fortune."

"But surely this little piece of straw can bring me no great fortune," thought the young man, and he was about to toss it on the roadside. Then he thought again, "No, I had better do exactly as the Kannon-Sama instructed me," so he carried the piece of straw carefully in his hand.

As he walked along the road, a horsefly began to buzz about his head. The young man picked up a stick and tried to shoo the fly away, but it would not stop bothering him. It buzzed and it buzzed, and it flew in little circles about his head. Finally the young man could bear it no longer. He cupped his hand, and with one big swoop, he caught the little horsefly. Then he strung it on the end of his stick with his piece of straw, and walked on.

Before long, a carriage carrying a noblewoman and her son to the temple came rolling toward him. The little boy was weary and hot, and was tired of sitting quietly in his carriage. He was fretting and crying, but he spied the horsefly buzzing on the end of the young man's stick.

"I want the little fly that's buzzing on the stick!" the little boy cried to his servant.

The servant approached the young man and said politely, "I wonder if you would be kind enough to give your stick to the little boy? He has grown weary from the long, hot ride, and this would make him very happy."

"Well, the fly is tied to the stick with a piece of straw which the goddess of the temple told me I must keep, but if it will make the little boy happy, I shall give it to him," said the young man.

"How very, very kind of you," the noblewoman said, as she leaned out of the carriage. "I'm afraid I have nothing with which I can repay you, except these three oranges." And she held out three large oranges on a beautiful white napkin.

The young man thanked the noblewoman, wrapped up the three oranges carefully, and walked on down the road. The sun was hot as it beat down on the dusty road. Before long, he saw a procession of men and women coming toward him. They were walking on either side of a beautiful carriage, and appeared to be the handmaidens and guards of the noblewoman inside. As the group walked by the young man, one of the young women suddenly grew faint and collapsed at the side of the road.

"Oh, I am so thirsty," she said weakly, and held her hand out for some water.

"Quickly, find some water," the guards shouted, but there was no water to be seen anywhere.

They called to the young man and asked if he could tell them where there might be some water.

"I fear there are no wells or streams nearby," said the young man. "But I have three oranges here. Give her the juice from these oranges to quench her thirst," and he handed his oranges to the guards. They quickly gave the young maiden the juice from the three oranges, and before long, she felt well enough to go on.

"If you had not come by and given me your oranges, I might have died here on this hot and dusty road," the maiden said to the young man. "I would give you anything to thank you, but I have only these three rolls of white silk. Take them and accept my thanks," she said, as she gave the rolls of silk to the young man.

The young man thanked her for the gift, and with the rolls of silk under his arm, he walked on down the road. "My goodness, one piece of straw brought me three oranges, and now my oranges have brought me three rolls of silk," thought the young man happily.

That night he found an inn where he could spend the night, and he gave the innkeeper one of the rolls of silk to pay for his room. Early the next morning, he started off down the road again. Toward noon, he saw a group of men on horseback cantering toward him. The horses held their heads up proudly, and whisked their long, shiny tails. The young man thought he had never seen such beautiful horses before, and looked at them longingly, for he had always wanted a horse for himself. Then, just as one of the noblemen rode past the young man, his horse suddenly faltered and fell to the ground. The men gathered about the animal and stroked its side and gave it water, but the horse would not move or raise its head.

"I'm afraid it's dead," said the nobleman sadly, and he took the saddle from the horse's back and the bit from its mouth. He then left one of his servants to care for the horse's remains, and rode off on another horse with his men.

The young man went up to the servant who was left to care for the horse. "He must have been a very fine horse," said the young man, as he looked down at the dead animal.

"Oh, yes, indeed he was," answered the servant. "He was such a valuable animal that even though many people offered large sums of money, the master would not think of selling him. It certainly is strange that he died so suddenly," he added, shaking his head.

"What are you going to do now?" the young man

asked.

"I can't let the horse just lie here beside the road. I really don't know what to do," answered the servant sadly.

"Well, if you like, I'll give you a roll of silk for the horse. Then you can return home and I shall take care of the horse," said the young man.

"What a strange person to want a dead horse," thought the servant, but he was happy to be on his way. "Why, that is a fine bargain, my friend," he said out loud, and he quickly took the roll of silk and hurried away before the young man should change his mind.

The young man then knelt down before the horse and prayed to the Goddess of Mercy that he might come to life again. "Oh, Kannon-Sama," he pleaded. "Please give life to this beautiful horse once more." Then, as he watched, the horse slowly opened its eyes. Then it slowly got to its feet, and before long, began to drink water and eat some oats. It shook its head, whisked its long, silky tail, and looked as good as new once again. The young man was so happy, he quickly climbed up on the horse's back and rode into the next village. There he spent the night at another inn, and used his last roll of silk to pay for his room.

The next day, he rode on his fine horse until he came

to the town of Toba. He knew he wasn't far from the big city of Kyoto when, suddenly, the young man thought of a problem. The nobleman was very well known in Kyoto, and many people probably knew his beautiful chestnut-colored horse. "It would never do if I should be accused of stealing the nobleman's horse," he thought, "for no one would believe the strange story of how the horse came to be mine."

So the young man decided he would sell the horse. Just then, he passed by the home of a family who appeared to be getting ready to leave on a journey. A wagon piled high with bags and boxes stood by the front gate. The young man called out to the man of the house, "Good sir, would you like to buy this horse from me?"

"My, what a beautiful horse. I certainly would like to buy it from you, but alas, I have no money," he answered.

Then the man came closer to look at the horse. It was more beautiful than any he had ever seen.

"Ah, what a pity I cannot buy such a fine animal," he said. "But wait, I know what I can do. I can give you three rice fields in exchange for your horse," said the man happily.

The young man thought for a moment. "Well—" he

began.

"What's more, since we are going away, I shall leave you the house, and you may live in it until we return," continued the man.

"That's a fair bargain indeed," said the young man. "The horse is yours!"

"In case we decide not to return, the house will be yours too," called the man, and soon he and his family rode off down the road with their wagon rumbling after them.

Now the young man found that one field of rice was plenty to keep himself well fed, so he rented out his other fields. As if by magic, the rice in his field grew and grew, until he had so much rice, he could sell many, many sacks each day. He grew richer and richer, and his purse grew fatter and fatter, and his luck seemed to grow with the years.

Many years went by, and still no one returned to the house, so the young man continued to live there and to raise fine crops of rice. His wealth increased tenfold, and he became an important man in the town. He married a beautiful young maiden of the village, and they had many lovely children. And there they lived happily for many years with their children, and their children's children in the little town of Toba.

So the one little piece of straw which the young man picked up so many years ago outside the temple gate had truly brought him great good fortune and happiness, just as the old man in his dream had said it would.

THE TONGUE-CUT SPARROW

THERE once lived a kind old man who had a very wicked and greedy wife. They lived alone except for a little pet sparrow which the old man kept in a cage in the kitchen.

One day the old man went into the woods to collect kindling for the fire while the old woman did her washing outside by the well. After she had scrubbed all her clothes, she went back into the house for the starch which she had made and left in the kitchen. But when she looked at the bowl in which she had left the starch, she found it empty.

"Who has stolen my starch?" cried the old woman angrily. "What wicked person has taken every bit of the starch I made for my nice clean clothes?"

The little sparrow heard the old woman shouting and called out, "What is it, old woman? What are you looking for?"

"My starch, my starch!" cried the old woman. "I left it right here in this bowl, and now every bit of it is gone!"

"Oh, my," said the sparrow sadly. "I didn't know that was your starch, for it was in the bowl in which I usually get my dinner. I thought it was for me and I ate it all up."

Now the old woman had never loved the sparrow as the old man did, so when she heard what he had done, she screamed at him in a rage. "You hateful sparrow! I will punish you for eating up all my lovely starch."

Then she snatched a pair of scissors and snipped off the poor little sparrow's tongue. "There, that will teach you to eat things that don't belong to you," she shouted. Then letting the sparrow out of the cage, she called, "Be off with you! I don't ever want to see you again." And she shooed the sparrow out of the door and into the woods.

When the old man came home from the woods, he looked for his little pet sparrow, but found the cage empty and forlorn.

"How now, where is my little sparrow? I brought home a nice juicy worm for him," he said to the old woman.

The old woman told him what had happened in the morning, and said crossly, "That is what he deserves for having stolen my starch."

"But he didn't do it on purpose," said the old man sadly. "You did a very cruel and unkind thing to my poor little sparrow," and he cried as bitterly as if he had lost his own son.

The very next morning, the old man arose bright and early and set out to look for his little sparrow. He looked into the bamboo thickets, but he heard only the chirping of a lonely cricket. He looked up at the blue, blue sky, but he saw only the white clouds drifting silently by. He wandered slowly toward the forest calling,

"Tongue-cut sparrow, where are you now?
Tongue-cut sparrow, where is your home?"

Far in the deep thickets the little sparrow heard the old man's voice calling him. He flew out quickly to greet him, saying, "Here I am, my kind friend and master. How good it is to see you again."

"Oh, my little sparrow!" exclaimed the old man happily. "I couldn't rest till I found you again. My wife did a very cruel thing to you, and I am so glad to find that you are safe and well."

The sparrow chirped happily, for he loved the old

man dearly. "Please come to see my little home," he said. "It was so kind of you to come to look for me."

The sparrow led the old man into his home, and wondered what he could do to entertain him. First, he spread his table with all sorts of strange and delicious foods, and the old man ate until he could eat no more. Then the sparrow called together his family and friends, and together they sang beautiful songs such as the old man had never heard before. Then they did the beautiful sparrow dance which most human beings are never permitted to see. The old man clapped his hands and rocked back and forth with glee, as the sparrows twirled and whirled in time to the lovely music.

At last the old man said, "Ah, I haven't had such a good time in many a year, but alas, it is growing dark, and I must think about returning home."

The little sparrow was sad to see the old man getting ready to leave and said, "If you cannot stay longer, I would at least like you to take a present home with you." Then he hurried into another room and came back with two golden chests. "Now one chest is very, very heavy and the other is very light. Which will you have, my friend?" asked the sparrow.

"Oh, thank you, the light one will be plenty for me," said the old man. "Besides, I am getting old, and I fear I could not carry the heavy one on my back."

So the old man took the lighter chest and carried it on his back. "Good-bye, good friend," he called to the sparrow. "I've had a lovely time indeed, and thank you so much for this fine present!"

"Please come back again soon," called the sparrow, and he stood at his door waving until the old man disappeared into the thick woods.

The golden moon was just beginning to climb up from behind the mountains as the old man trudged wearily back to his little home. Now the old woman had been waiting very impatiently for the old man, and when she saw him coming through the gate she called out crossly, "Well, old man, what have you been doing? Where have you been? I have been waiting all the long day for you!"

"Now, now, don't be cross," said the old man. "I have had such a lovely visit with my little pet sparrow. He gave me all kinds of delicious food and drink, and his friends did a beautiful dance for me. Then, when I was ready to leave for home, he even gave me a lovely present."

"A present?" asked the old woman. "Quickly, let me see it!"

"You see," explained the old man, "he had two chests,

one which was heavy, and the other which was light. I chose the lighter one for I am much too old to carry a heavy bundle on my back."

Now the old woman was so anxious to see the present, she didn't even bother to make a cup of hot tea for the tired old man. Instead she snatched greedily at the chest and tore off the lid. When she saw what was inside, she could scarcely believe her eyes. The chest was filled with gold and silver; with beautiful sparkling diamonds and creamy white pearls; with rubies and emeralds, and many, many glittering and precious stones. There were beautiful silken *kimonos* and lovely *obis* of golden brocade.

"What lovely, wonderful gifts," said the old man happily. But the old woman only said, "Old man, why didn't you take the heavier chest? We could have gotten twice as many jewels and twice as much gold. You are a silly old man to come home with the smaller and lighter chest."

"But, my dear, do not be so greedy! This is more than we shall ever need. Is this not plenty for you and me?" asked the old man.

"No, indeed it isn't," said the old woman. "I am going right back to the sparrow's house and get the heavier chest now."

The old man begged the old woman not to do such a

foolish thing, but she would not listen to him. "I shall be back in a short while," she said, and hurried out of the house toward the woods.

She walked down the lonely path calling,

"Tongue-cut sparrow, where are you now?
Tongue-cut sparrow, where do you live?"

At last she came upon the small house of the sparrow and knocked on the door. "Tongue-cut sparrow, is this where you live?" she asked in a sweet voice.

The little sparrow opened the door and was surprised indeed to see the cross old woman. He was a very polite sparrow, however, so he said, "Good evening, old woman, won't you come in?"

"No, no, I can't come in. I am in a very great hurry," answered the old woman.

"Won't you come in just for a cup of tea?" asked the sparrow.

"No, no, I don't want any tea or any food. I don't even want to see your beautiful dance. Just give me a present to take home with me. That will do," said the rude old woman.

"Very well then," said the sparrow, and he again brought out two golden chests. "One is heavy, but the other is light," said the sparrow. "Which one will you have?"

"I am younger and stronger than the old man," said the woman. "Give me the heavy one. I can manage very well."

So the old woman hoisted the heavy chest onto her back and set out for home. As she walked on, the chest seemed to grow heavier and heavier with each step.

"Oh, my poor back," moaned the old woman, but when she thought of all the gold and jewels which must be inside, she smiled happily and walked on. Soon she was so eager to see the treasures inside the chest, she couldn't wait until she got home. "I must see what is inside," she said to herself. "I'll just take a little peek right now."

So she lowered the heavy chest to the ground and lifted the cover very carefully. She looked inside, expecting to see twice as many beautiful things as she had seen in the first chest, but there wasn't a single jewel there. When the old woman saw what was in the chest, she screamed in terror and fell to the ground. For this chest was filled with snakes and caterpillars, giant toads and poison spiders, and a huge three-eyed monster. They slithered and slid around and began to crawl out over the sides. They climbed on the old woman and swarmed about her head until she screamed and shrieked for help.

"Save me! Save me!" she cried with all her strength, but no one came to help her. At last she tore herself away from the horrible creatures and ran home as fast as her legs would carry her. When she got there she told the old man what had happened, and of the terrible creatures in the big chest.

"I'm not at all surprised," said the old man. "You see, that is what comes of being so greedy. Perhaps this has taught you a good lesson."

The old woman hung her head in shame and answered, "Indeed it has, old man. I shall never be greedy or unkind again."

And from that day on, the old woman truly kept her word. She was never greedy again, and before long she became just as good and kind as the kind old man.

THE PRINCESS AND THE
FISHERMAN

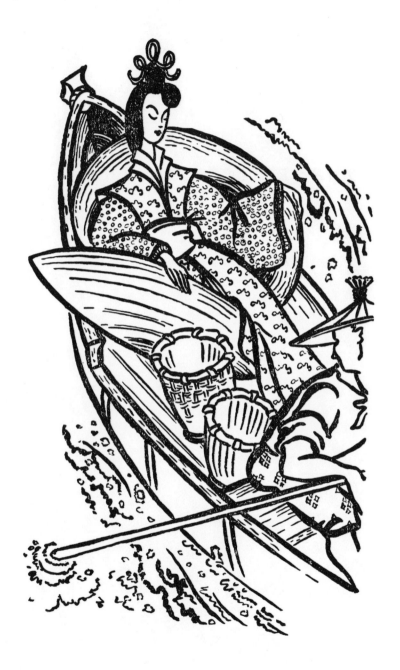

THE PRINCESS AND THE
FISHERMAN

LONG, long ago, in a small village in Japan, there lived a young fisherman with his mother in a cottage by the sea. They were poor, but they were good and kindly people, and were loved by all in the village. Each morning the fisherman walked to the sea and rowed out over the deep blue waters. Each night he returned with a boat full of shiny, big fish which he sold at the village market.

Now one bright and sunny morning, the fisherman set out to sea as he did each day, anxious to bring in a big catch. He rowed far out over the sparkling water, threw out his line, and waited for the fish to bite. He sat back and looked up at the cloudless blue sky. The sun felt warm and the salt air smelled good.

"Ah, an excellent day for fishing," he sighed happily,

but he had spoken too soon. Before long, a frown spread across his face, for although he waited and waited, not a single fish came to nibble on his line. He rowed from one spot to another, casting his line and waiting patiently, but not one fish seemed to be in the sea that day.

As morning turned to noon, and afternoon to dusk, the tired fisherman looked sadly at the empty baskets which stood in the bottom of his boat. Alas, he thought, they would have to go back empty, just as they had come, and he would have nothing to show for his day's labors. The sun was beginning to slip slowly into the sea when at last the fisherman decided to turn his boat around and row toward the shore.

Suddenly there was a tiny tug at his line. "Oh-ho!" shouted the fisherman. "I will have at least one fish for our supper tonight." He quickly pulled up his line and looked eagerly to see what he had caught. There, to his great disappointment, dangled one small clam. The fisherman was ready to throw it back into the sea, but how strange it was to catch a clam on a fishhook, he thought. He decided to keep it, thinking it might taste good in his soup that night. He tossed it carelessly into one of his empty baskets and headed for home.

He rowed slowly because, for some strange reason,

the oars felt heavy and clumsy in his hands, and the boat seemed to grow heavier and heavier as he rowed on. The fisherman glanced back over his shoulder, for he knew the baskets were empty and should not be so heavy. All at once he stopped rowing and almost dropped his oars into the sea, for the little clam which he had just caught was growing larger and larger and larger until it was almost too big for his small boat.

The fisherman was so startled he could scarcely think or talk.

"Whhhhy, what is this?" he exclaimed. "Stop growing or you will upset my boat!" he shouted. Slowly the shell began to open, and he could see a bright light shining from inside. It grew brighter and brighter till he could no longer see. He blinked and rubbed his eyes and shook his head. "I must be dreaming," he murmured, but when he looked up, there stood the most beautiful young woman he had ever seen.

"Good heavens! Who are you? Where did you come from?" he stammered.

She looked like all the pictures of princesses that he had seen in books, but she was not smiling as they usually did. Instead she looked lonely and sad.

"Alas," she sighed. "I do not know who I am or where I am bound. I am without a name or a home. Please, kind fisherman, will you not let me come to your home with you?"

"Oh, indeed I will," said the fisherman and, picking up his oars, he quickly rowed for the shore.

They walked along the smooth, white sand toward the fisherman's cottage, and when they came near, the fisherman ran ahead to tell his mother of this wonderful clamshell and the beautiful maiden.

"My, my," cried the old woman. "By all means, we must welcome her to our home." Then she called, "Come in, my dear. If you are willing to stay in a home as humble as ours, you are more than welcome to stay as long as you wish."

"Oh, you are both very kind," said the lovely maiden. She was smiling now, and her eyes sparkled with happiness. The fisherman looked at her, and knew she was a real princess.

Before long, word spread throughout the countryside that a true princess lived at the home of the fisherman and his old mother. Everyone wanted a glimpse of this wonderful princess who had emerged from the giant clamshell. And soon many people came from far and wide, over the rough dirt roads, bearing gifts of rice and flax. Old people and young people, children and babies in the arms of their mothers—all came to see the princess. The gifts of rice and flax began to pile high in the house of the fisherman.

One day the princess carefully selected the best of the flax, pulled the threads out long and fine, and said, "Now I shall weave a beautiful piece of cloth from this flax. But before I begin I have one request to make of you."

"Why, what is it?" asked the old woman and her son.

"You must never enter the room in which I am weaving, for I do not want you to see the cloth until it is completed," she replied.

And so the princess sat alone in a little room, weaving the linen threads upon an old wooden loom. All day the woman could hear the clickety-clack-swish, clickety-clack-swish of the loom as the princess wove her cloth. Many times the old woman and the fisherman wished to have just a glimpse of the cloth, but remembering what the princess had said, they did not go into the room. On the twenty-eighth day after the princess had begun her weaving, she opened the door of the little room. She smiled as she called to the fisherman and his mother, "Now, my friends, at last I have finished weaving my cloth. Come in and see what I have made."

They hurried into the room, anxious to see what the

princess had hidden from them for so long. There they saw a large cloth with a design more strange than anything they had ever seen, and with colors more beautiful than the very sunset itself.

"Ah, it is just as lovely as you are," said the fisherman, as he and his mother looked at the strangely beautiful cloth. The old woman felt the fine cloth with her workworn fingers and sighed, "Never have I seen anything so beautiful or so fine."

"Now," said the princess to the fisherman, "I would like you to take the cloth into town and sell it for no less than 3000 yen."

So early the next morning the fisherman set out for the big city to sell the princess' cloth. He traveled from one shop to another, showing each merchant the lovely piece of weaving.

"It is by far the most beautiful thing I have ever seen," said one. "It looks like something from another world," said another. "I would like ten pieces just like this one," said still another. But when the fisherman told them that he wanted 3000 yen for it, they shook their heads sadly. "My dear young man," they said, "we are just poor merchants, we are not kings. We cannot afford to pay 3000 yen for one piece of cloth."

And so the fisherman went from one merchant to another throughout the city, but everywhere he was given the same answer. Before long the shopkeepers began to light their lamps and close their soft sliding doors, and still he had not sold the cloth. The fisherman wondered what he could say to the princess, as he sadly turned toward his home with the cloth still wrapped in a silken *furoshiki.*

Just then, he looked down the road and saw a wealthy old man traveling with many, many servants. The old man beckoned to the fisherman, and the fisherman quickly showed him the beautiful linen cloth.

The old man smiled until his face was all wrinkles and little lines. "Well, well, my good man, this certainly is the most beautiful cloth I have ever seen, and I have lived a good many years. It's a sight for my tired old eyes," said the old man as he stroked the princess' cloth. "I would be willing to pay a pretty price for anything as lovely as this."

"I ask for 3000 yen, good sir," said the fisherman in a soft voice, for he was afraid the old man would say the same thing as all the others.

But the old man surprised him. "Ah, a cheap price for anything so beautiful. Come, bring it to my home for me," he said.

So the fisherman followed the old man to his home.

When he reached the gate, he saw that he was about to enter a magnificent golden palace. From somewhere he could hear the playing of sweet music, and although there was no breeze, soft pink blossoms were drifting here and there, leaving a lovely scent in the air.

Then the fisherman was served a delicious dinner, with more wonderful dishes than he had ever dreamed of, and while he ate he was entertained by music and dancing. The fisherman had never had such a good time. When at last he could eat no more, the old man called one of his servants.

"See that 3000 yen are delivered to the home of this young man," he said. Then, as if his task were completed, he rose, lifted his hand, and beckoned to a snowy white cloud up in the sky. The cloud slowly drifted down toward the old man and the surprised fisherman. When it reached the old man it stopped and hovered at his feet. The old man stepped onto it, waved his hand, and the cloud slowly rose again into the heavens.

The fisherman was so surprised he could scarcely speak. "I knew he was no ordinary mortal," he whispered to himself, and bowed down very low, for he didn't know what else he should do. When he looked up, the old man and the cloud were gone and the palace had disappeared. Only the pink blossoms fluttered softly in the air.

The fisherman left quickly and hurried for home, wondering if the 3000 yen would really be there. When he arrived, he saw three bags of gold waiting for him on his front step.

He hurried to tell the princess of his good fortune, but before he could speak she said, "Wasn't it fortunate that you could sell my cloth?" She seemed to know just what had happened before the fisherman could say anything.

"I have you to thank for our good fortune," said the fisherman. "Somehow our luck has truly turned since the day you came."

"Ah, yes, and that is why I can leave you now," said the princess.

Both the fisherman and his mother cried out together, "But why? We want you to stay with us always."

"Alas, I wish I could," said the princess, "for I have been very happy here, but my task is done and I must return. You see, I was sent down by the gods to bring you happiness and good fortune because you have been such fine and kindly people. Now my task is completed and I must return." Then, waving her hand, the beautiful princess disappeared into the sky, just as suddenly as she had first appeared.

From that day on, the fisherman and his mother were never poor again. They continued to be good, kind, hard-working people, and were loved, as always, by everyone in the village.

THE OLD MAN OF THE FLOWERS

THE OLD MAN OF THE
FLOWERS

ONCE upon a time, in a village in Japan, there lived a kind old man and woman with their little dog, Shiro. They called him Shiro because he was as white as snow. Since they had no children, they treated Shiro just like their own child, and took him everywhere they went. When the old man went out into his garden to tend the little dwarfed pine trees, Shiro ran along at his side. When the old man dug up turnips and sweet potatoes from his vegetable garden, Shiro would carry them back to the old woman. He was a very wise dog indeed, and the old man and woman loved him dearly.

One day, as the old man worked in his vegetable plot, Shiro sniffed about in the corners of the garden. Suddenly, he ran to the old man and began to tug at the sleeve of his *kimono*.

"Here, here, Shiro, what are you doing? You'll tear my clothes!" said the old man. But Shiro would not stop. He barked and tugged as hard as he could, until finally the old man decided to see what was the matter. He followed Shiro to a corner of the garden and there Shiro began to scratch the ground and bark, "Wuf-wuf, dig here! Wuf-wuf, dig here!"

"Dig here? In this bare corner, Shiro?" asked the old man.

"Wuf-wuf!" answered Shiro, wagging his tail happily.

"Well, just as you say," said the old man, and he began to dig in the hard, dry soil. Down went the shovel, and up came the dirt! "Heave ho, heave ho. . . . Yoi-sho, yoi-sho!" sang the old man as he dug. Suddenly he heard a clink-clank, clink-clank, as his shovel struck something hard. He looked closely, and to his surprise, he saw hundreds of sparkling gold coins.

"My, my, what is this!" he exclaimed happily, and then he ran home to tell the old woman of the treasure he had discovered. The old woman hurried to the spot with him, and together they filled a large sack full of coins, and carried it back to the house.

"We will never be poor again," said the old man happily. "And we owe it all to Shiro!"

"Yes, yes, we never would have discovered the treasure without him," said the old woman.

Then they both stroked Shiro's head tenderly, and they gave him a big dinner of rice and fish which he liked so well.

Now there was a very greedy and wicked man who lived next door to the kind old man and woman. When he heard of the treasure which his neighbor had discovered, he quickly ran over to borrow Shiro, for he wanted the dog to do the same thing for him.

He bowed very low and said to the kind old man, "Would you be good enough to let me borrow Shiro for the day?"

"Why, of course," answered the kind old man, for he was a very generous person indeed.

The greedy man took Shiro by the collar and hurried with him out into his own garden.

"Now show me where my treasure is!" he shouted at Shiro, as he dragged him about the garden. But Shiro would do nothing. "Bark quickly and show me the spot, or I will beat you with my shovel," he cried.

Poor little Shiro became so frightened that at last he weakly cried, "Wuf-wuf, dig here." The greedy man then began to dig just as quickly as he could. The shovel went down and the dirt flew up. Suddenly he heard a clink-clank as his shovel struck something hard. "Ah, here is my treasure," said the man greedily, but when he reached down to gather the coins, he found only a mass of dirty rocks and pebbles.

"You have tricked me!" he shouted angrily at Shiro. "And for that you deserve to die!" Then he struck Shiro on the head with his shovel and killed him.

Now the kind old man knew nothing of all this, so when dusk came and still Shiro had not returned, he decided to go after him. He knocked on the door of his neighbor's house and called, "I've come for Shiro, for it is time for his supper."

The wicked man came to the door and said with a scowl, "Oh, have you come for that worthless dog of yours? He tricked me and gave me rocks instead of coins, so I killed him."

"Oh, my poor little Shiro," cried the kind old man. He ran out to the garden and picked up the body of his little dog. Then he gently carried it home. The old man and woman were very, very sad. They buried Shiro in their garden and planted a little pine tree on his grave. Before long, this little tree grew so large that the old man could no longer put his arms around its trunk.

One day the old woman said, "Let us make something

fine and useful from the wood of this pine tree so that we will always have something with which to remember Shiro."

"Ah, a fine idea," agreed the old man. "What shall I make from the wood?"

"I need a new bowl in which to grind rice flour," answered the old woman. "Then I will be able to make some rice cakes, which Shiro liked so well, for our New Year's celebration."

"Then that is what I shall make for you," said the old man, and he cut down the pine tree and made a beautiful big bowl for the old woman. He polished the wood until it gleamed, and then he said, "Now I will help you grind some rice flour, and you can make some rice cakes."

Together the old man and woman began to pound and grind the rice in their new bowl. Suddenly they both stopped, for something very strange was happening. The amount of rice in the bowl seemed to be growing and growing, until soon it was overflowing onto the floor. Before they could stop it, the floor was covered with rice, and soon it began to flow out into their yard.

"Just see what is happening!" cried the old woman. "We shall never have to worry about going hungry, for this is enough rice to last us all our lives."

"Indeed it is," said the old man. "Why, this bowl must be filled with magic! Or perhaps Shiro is still helping us!"

The old man and woman had just gathered up all their rice and stored it away carefully when they heard a knock on their door. It was their greedy neighbor who had seen what had happened.

Once again he bowed very politely and asked, "I wonder if I may borrow your lovely new bowl for a day or two?"

"Why, of course you may," answered the generous old man, and so his neighbor carried off the beautiful new bowl. Quickly he put in some rice, and began to grind it into flour. "Give me rice! Lots of rice!" he sang out as he ground the rice. He watched the bowl anxiously, waiting for it to overflow with rice, but nothing happened. At last something seemed to bubble up from the bottom of the bowl. The greedy man rubbed his hands together and waited to catch the rice, but instead of rice, dirty rocks and pebbles came tumbling out of the bowl. Soon his house and garden were filled with them. The greedy man shrieked with rage, and threw the new bowl onto the hard floor where it broke into many pieces.

"Ah, you worthless wooden bowl!" he shouted. "I

will use you for kindling wood!" And he threw the lovely bowl into his stove and set fire to it.

When the kind old man went to get his bowl, his wicked neighbor said, "Oh, have you come for that bowl? It was useless, so I burned it in my stove."

"Oh, but we made that bowl in memory of our dear Shiro," said the kind old man. He felt very sad, but he knew it was useless to argue with his neighbor so he simply asked, "If you cannot give me my bowl, will you at least let me have the ashes that remain from it?"

"Take them, for they are of no use to me," answered the wicked man.

And so the kind old man scooped out the ashes that had fallen beneath the grating of the stove and carried them home in a barrel. As he walked home, with the barrel under his arm, a breeze came along and began to carry the ashes away. They scattered about in the air and fell on the barren branches of the cherry trees that stood along the road. Then something very wonderful happened. As soon as the ashes came to rest on a branch, that branch became covered with beautiful pink blossoms. The old man could scarcely believe his eyes. "It is a miracle! A true miracle!" Then he hurried home to tell the old woman what had happened.

As he told her about the ashes that brought forth

lovely cherry blossoms on the barren trees, he had a wonderful idea. "Just think what I could do!" he said to her. "I could go about the countryside covering all the bare trees with beautiful blossoms. How happy everyone would be to see the trees blossoming at this time of year!" The old man chuckled with glee at the thought, and the old woman hastened to make a little red cap and a blue quilted jacket for the old man to wear on his journey.

When all was ready, the old man put on his bright new clothes, strapped the barrel of ashes on his back, and set out on his journey. He walked along the road, scattering ashes on all the trees and singing in a loud, clear voice,

> "I will make the flowers bloom,
>   Old man of the flowers!
> On dead branches, flowers gay,
>   Old man of the flowers!"

He smiled cheerfully, as beautiful flowers blossomed forth on all the dry, brown branches. It seemed just like spring again.

As he walked along, he saw a cloud of dust coming toward him. When it came closer, he could see that it was a long procession of men on horseback. Soon he knew that it was the prince riding back to his palace.

"Well, well, what has happened?" asked the prince looking about. "These trees should not be in bloom in the middle of winter!" Then he saw what the old man was doing, and he heard his little song. "Well, my good man," he called to the kind old man. "You have made the countryside beautiful with your magical ashes, and you will bring much happiness to all my people." Turning to his servant he said, "See that this old man of the flowers is given much food, clothing, and money. He deserves a reward for such a good deed."

"Oh, thank you, sir! Thank you very much," said the old man happily. Then he hurried home to tell the old woman of the wonderful good fortune that had befallen him.

Now when their greedy neighbor heard of the many rewards which the prince had bestowed upon the kind old man, he was even more envious than before. "I too must get a reward from the prince," he said to himself, and he hastily gathered up the ashes that remained in his stove. He too put on a red cap and a blue quilted jacket just as the kind old man had done, and singing the same song, he set out on the road. Soon he saw the prince approaching with his men, so he began to scatter his ashes all about and to sing in a loud voice,

"I will make the flowers bloom,
Old man of the flowers!
On dead branches, flowers gay,
Old man of the flowers!"

But as he threw the ashes, they did not turn into beautiful flowers at all. Instead, they blew right into the eyes and noses of the prince and all his men.

"What is the meaning of this!" shouted the prince angrily. "What do you think you are doing?" he called to the greedy man, as he wiped the ashes from his face.

"But, sir, I am the old man of the flowers. I was only trying to make the trees blossom again," murmured the greedy neighbor.

"You are not the true old man of the flowers. You are only trying to do as he did, so that you too will be rewarded," retorted the prince. "For being such a greedy and wicked man, you shall be punished and sent to jail." As the prince spoke, his servants rushed toward the wicked man and tied him securely so he could not escape.

"Have pity on me! Please let me go!" he cried, but it was of no use.

And so the greedy neighbor was taken away to be punished for his many wicked deeds, while the kind old man and woman lived happily ever after.

ISUN BOSHI, THE ONE-INCH LAD

ISUN BOSHI, THE ONE-INCH LAD

LONG, long ago, when the city of Osaka was still known as Naniwa, there lived in its outskirts a man and woman. Their one wish in life was to have a child of their own, and one day this wish was granted. They had a little son, but this son was no ordinary boy. He was very, very special indeed, for he was no bigger than his mother's little finger! In fact, he could sit right down on the palm of her hand. The man and woman were surprised to have such a tiny son, but they were very happy to have a child of their own.

"Let us call him Isun Boshi," said his mother, for that meant One-Inch Lad.

"Yes, that is a good name," agreed his father. "I will make a special little bed of bamboo and twine for our little Isun Boshi."

"And I will sew him some tiny clothes," said his mother.

The man and woman took good care of their little boy, and he was a healthy, happy child even though he never grew much taller. Although Isun Boshi was very small, he could do many things to help his mother and father. He helped his mother find the pins and needles which dropped out of her sewing basket; and he often went out to the woods with his father to gather kindling for the kitchen stove. He picked up all the tiny twigs which they used to start the fire, and carried them home in a little bundle on his back. His mother and father often said to each other, "My, what a good and helpful son we have!"

One day when Isun Boshi was fifteen years old, he came to his parents and said, "Mother and Father, now that I am fifteen, I wish to go to Kyoto, the capital of our country, and become a great person. Please say that I may go," he pleaded.

"Kyoto is a big, big city, my son," said his father.

"And it is far from home," added his mother. They both shook their heads and opened their lips to say no, but little Isun Boshi begged so hard that at last they gave their consent.

His mother took a long, slim needle from her sewing

basket and slipped it into the hollow of a piece of straw. "Here is a sword and scabbard for you, my son," she said, as she tied the needle and straw about Isun Boshi's waist. "You may need this to protect yourself some day."

Then his father hurried to the cupboard and brought down a little red lacquer soup bowl, and a pair of bamboo chopsticks. "Look at the fine boat I have found for you, Isun Boshi!" he exclaimed. "And a fine pair of oars to go with it!"

Isun Boshi was so excited he could hardly eat his supper that evening, and all through the night he dreamed of the long journey he would start on the following day. When the sun had just begun to rise over the rooftops of the village of Naniwa, Isun Boshi was up and ready to start off. With his sword at his side and a lunch tucked under his arm, Isun Boshi was ready to leave. His mother and father walked with him to the edge of the Yodo River to watch him sail off for the city of Kyoto.

"Good-bye, Mother! Good-bye, Father!" called Isun Boshi. "I shall send for you both soon." Then he jumped into the little red bowl and began to pull on the oars. Soon he felt himself sailing away from the shore, and his little boat went bobbing out over the blue water.

"Good-bye, son!" called his father.

"Be careful, little Isun Boshi," called his mother.

"Heave ho, heave ho! To the capital I will go!" sang Isun Boshi, as he rowed further and further away from the two small figures standing at the water's edge. And so Isun Boshi was off on his long journey. All day long he rowed under the smiling sun, and when night fell, he pulled his boat in among the tall green reeds that lined the shore. Slowly his head began to nod, and soon he was dreaming of his home in Naniwa. Only the big full moon that looked down among the reeds knew that little Isun Boshi slept there in a tiny red soup bowl.

Each morning Isun Boshi rose with the sun, and rowed closer and closer to the capital. One day, as he was rowing along, he saw black clouds scowling at him from a dark sky. Before he could row for the shore the wind began to blow; big drops of rain came tumbling down, and the river swirled angrily with foaming waves and whitecaps. Whish! Whish! His little bowl rolled and tossed from one side to the other! With all his might, Isun Boshi tried to steer his boat toward the shore, but the wind pitched it about like a small red leaf. "Help! Help!" cried Isun Boshi, but no one answered. The wind just howled louder and louder, and the waves lashed out angry wet fingers at the little red boat. Isun Boshi was about to give up all hope when suddenly he looked up and saw a boat loaded with kindling wood coming toward him. Before he could cry out again, someone bent down and scooped him up, bowl and all, right into the safe big boat. Isun Boshi sighed with relief, and then fell asleep exhausted. When he woke up, he saw the face of a kind old man peering down into his own. He looked about and saw that he was on the palm of the man's hand.

"Well, well, little one, just where did you think you were going in that tiny boat?" asked the kind old man.

"I'm going to the capital to become a great person," answered Isun Boshi.

"Now that is a fine ambition indeed, but you surely couldn't have gotten there in that little soup bowl," said the old man with a smile. "Let me help you to start on your career by taking you to the shores of the capital in my boat," he added.

"Oh, thank you, sir," said Isun Boshi.

And so the two of them sailed on down the Yodo River towards Kyoto—the kind old man of the big boat, and the small boy from Naniwa.

When at last they reached the shores of Kyoto, the old man lifted Isun Boshi down onto the wharf and said, "Good luck, little One-Inch Lad. I am sure you will become a great man some day!"

"Thank you, sir," said Isun Boshi. "I shall never, never forget how you helped me." He bowed low to the old man, and then set off to see the big city. My, but there were so many long legs striding down the street! Clop-clop, clop-clop, went the sound of hundreds of wooden *getas* along the cobbled street. Little Isun Boshi had to leap from space to space to keep from being trampled upon. He had never seen so many people before!

Isun Boshi looked into every doorway with his eyes shining and wide. Here was a shop selling tiny bright-hued fish swimming about in crystal clear bowls; here was another selling beautiful silken *kimonos* and bright *obis* flecked with gold and silver threads; and here was still another selling row upon row of gleaming rice bowls, tiny teacups, and shiny lacquer trays. Such wonderful sights he had never seen!

Before he knew it, he had wandered straight to the gateway of a beautiful mansion in the middle of the city. It was the home of one of Kyoto's greatest nobles. Isun Boshi squeezed through one of the crevices in the tall wooden fence that surrounded the large house, and found himself in a lovely green garden. There was a large pond in the center, with a little red footbridge that curved its way over the smooth water. Isun Boshi laughed happily and ran over the little bridge. This brought him to a neat path of flagstones which led up to the low veranda of the house.

Isun Boshi thought for a moment and decided that this was where he would like to live. He called in a loud voice, "Hello! Is anybody home?" He listened quietly, but not a sound did he hear. He called again, "Isn't anybody home? Hello . . . Hello . . . Hello!"

Suddenly he heard the soft swish of a long *kimono*, and the sound of padded feet. "That's strange," said a loud, deep voice. "I thought I heard someone calling me." This was the great noble who lived in the beautiful mansion. He looked all about the garden, and up and down the walk, and then, shaking his head, he turned to go inside.

Isun Boshi shouted at the top of his voice, "Look down at your feet. Here I am! Here I am!" The noble stopped and glanced down toward his feet, and there he saw Isun Boshi looking like a little doll.

"Well, well, well!" said the noble, stooping down to pick up Isun Boshi. He put him on his outspread fan and looked at him with smiling eyes. "Who are you, and where did you come from, little one?" he asked.

"My name is Isun Boshi, sir, and I have come all the way from Naniwa. I wish to become a great person like you. Please let me stay here with you and become one of your followers," said Isun Boshi.

"Well, you seem to be a good and ambitious lad," said

165

the noble kindly. "I will grant you your wish. You shall stay with me and be one of my followers!"

Isun Boshi was so happy he could only murmur, "Thank you, sir, thank you very, very much!"

And so Isun Boshi became a member of the noble's household, and before long he was everyone's favorite. The noble's beautiful daughter, Haru Hime, which means Princess of Spring, taught Isun Boshi how to read and write each day, so that he could become a great scholar. In return, he helped the princess in many little ways, just as he used to help his mother in Naniwa. Everyone in the noble's mansion came to love Isun Boshi dearly, for he worked hard, studied hard, and kept everyone happy with his cheerful ways. And so Isun Boshi spent several happy years in the home of the great noble.

One beautiful spring day, the princess called Isun Boshi and all her handmaids about her, and said, "We cannot stay home on such a lovely day. Come along, let us all go out to the park!" There was a scurry for parasols and kerchiefs, and soon a procession started out the garden gate. All the handmaids clustered about the princess, holding their parasols high to shield her from the sun, while little Isun Boshi ran along at her feet.

When they reached the park, Isun Boshi saw beautiful flowers and cherry blossoms everywhere. "Some day I will bring my mother and father here too," he thought. "I have been in the capital for many years, and soon I must call for them."

Isun Boshi was dreaming of his home in Naniwa, when suddenly he heard the handmaids screaming. They all began to run out of the park just as fast as they could go. He looked up to see what was the matter, and to his horror saw a huge red ogre rushing out of the woods at the edge of the park. He was running toward the princess with a fierce scowl on his ugly face.

"Help me, help me," called the princess, but all her maids ran away from her. They were too frightened to help. When Isun Boshi saw this, he reached for his little sword and ran at the ugly ogre.

"I'm coming, Haru Hime!" he called.

When the ogre saw little Isun Boshi, he roared angrily, "Ha, what is this little thing! A dainty morsel he will be for me," and with one scoop he picked Isun Boshi up off the ground and popped him right into his mouth! Down . . . down . . . down went little Isun Boshi into the ogre's stomach. My, but it was dark down there. When he came to a stop he drew out the little needle that his mother had given him long ago. Then he began to prick, prick, prick, all over the ogre's stomach and the ogre began to groan and shriek.

"What is happening to my stomach?" he cried. "Stop! Stop!" He doubled up in pain, and forgot all about the princess.

Now Isun Boshi crawled slowly upward. He put aside his little sword and began to blow and tickle, so the ogre would sneeze.

"AAAAAAAH–CHOOOOOOOOO!!!" bellowed the ogre, and out popped Isun Boshi from his mouth. The ogre was blinded by the tears that streamed down his face as he sneezed and coughed and shrieked. He quickly ran back into the woods from where he had come, never to bother anyone again.

"You saved my life, little Isun Boshi," said the princess. "And how brave you were, when all the others ran away!"

"It wasn't very hard to do," said Isun Boshi, smiling happily.

Suddenly they both noticed that the ogre had dropped something when he ran away. It was a good-luck charm.

"Oh, Isun Boshi, that is a charm for luck. They say that if anyone shakes it three times and makes a wish, his wish will come true. Shake it, and make a wish, Isun Boshi!" cried the princess.

Isun Boshi took the little charm in his hand and gave

it three shakes—one, two, three! Then he made a wish.
And what do you suppose happened? Isun Boshi suddenly changed into a tall young man, just as handsome
as you please!

"Oh, Isun Boshi, you are taller than I am!" exclaimed
the princess happily. "Come, let's hurry home and tell
Father."

They hurried home to the beautiful mansion, and
together they told the noble how Isun Boshi had saved
the princess from the ugly red ogre of the woods.

"You have shown yourself to be a brave young man,"
said the noble kindly. "I think you are well worthy of
having half of all my lands, and my daughter, Haru
Hime, for your bride."

And so, before long, Isun Boshi became a great person
in the capital. Everyone knew of his brave deeds and
of his kindness to others. He called his mother and
father from Naniwa, and together they all lived happily
ever after.

Guide to Pronunciation

Susano soo-sa-no
Taro ta-ro
Tamanoi ta-ma-no-ee
Toba toh-ba
Urashima oo-ra-shee-ma
Usagi to Wani oo-sa-gi toh wa-nee
Yamato ya-ma-toh
Yamato no Orochi ya-ma-toh no o-ro-chee
Yodo yo-do

Note: These words should be pronounced without accenting any of the syllables.

GLOSSARY

akano gohan	ah-ka-no go-hahn	rice cooked with small red (Azuki) beans; made for happy occasions such as birthdays, weddings and festivals
furoshiki	foo-ro-shee-kee	a square cloth used to wrap and carry articles
geta	geh-ta	a wooden clog
hibachi	hee-ba-chee	a brazier
kimono	kee-mo-no	a Japanese dress
maga-tama	ma-ga-ta-ma	a claw-shaped stone bead used in necklaces worn by royalty
obi	o-bee	a sash
oya-oya	o-ya-o-ya	an exclamation
San	sahn	this is often added to a person's name as

		a more polite way of speaking to him; it is very much like the Mr. or Mrs. we add to a person's name
tai	**ta-ee**	a fish baked for special happy occasions
tatami	ta-ta-mee	woven straw mats placed on floors
yoi-sho	yoi-sho	an exclamation

GUIDE TO PRONUNCIATION

Bumbuku Chagama   boom-boo-koo cha-ga-ma
Chuko   choo-ko
Hamaguri Hime   ha-ma-goo-ree hee-meh
Hanasaka Jii   ha-na-sa-ka jii
Haru Hime   ha-roo hee-meh
Hase   ha-seh
Inaba   ee-na-ba
Ippon no Wara   ip-pon no wa-ra
Isun Boshi   ees-soon bo-shee
Izumo   ee-zoo-mo
Kannon-Sama   kahn-non sa-ma
Kaguya Hime   ka-goo-ya hee-meh
Kobutori Jii-san   ko-boo-to-ree jee-sahn
Kyoto   kyo-toh
Momotaro   mo-mo-ta-ro
Naniwa   na-nee-wa
Nezumi no Yomeiri   neh-zoo-mee no yo-meh-eeri
Oki   o-kee
Osaka   oh-sa-ka
Shiro   shee-ro
Shitakiri Suzume   shee-ta-keeri soo-zoo-meh

Yoshiko Uchida was born in Alameda, California and grew up in Berkeley, the locale of her recent trilogy, *A Jar Of Dreams, The Best Bad Thing* and *The Happiest Ending.* She earned her BA with honors from the University of California, Berkeley, and has a Masters in Education from Smith College.

She began writing when she was ten years old, creating small books out of brown wrapping paper in which to write her stories. She is now the author of twenty-five published books for young people and has won many awards for her work, including a Distinguished Service Award from the University of Oregon.

Her published work for adults includes many articles and short stories as well as a novel, *Picture Bride,* and a non-fiction book, *Desert Exile,* which tells of her family's World War II internment experiences when they were among the 120,000 Japanese Americans imprisoned by the US government.

Although many of her earlier books were about Japan and its young people, (including three collections of Japanese folk tales, *The Dancing Kettle, The Magic Listening Cap* and *The Sea of Gold*), her recent work focuses on the Japanese American experience in California.

She says of her work, "I hope to give young Asians a sense of their own history, but at the same time, I want to dispel the stereotypic image held by many non-Asians about the Japanese Americans and write about them as real people. I also want to convey the sense of hope and strength of spirit of the first generation Japanese Americans. Beyond that," she adds, "I want to celebrate our common humanity."